MOBBED UP 4

King Rio

Lock Down Publications and Ca$h Presents

Mobbed Up 4
A Novel by *King Rio*

Lock Down Publications

P.O. Box 944
Stockbridge, Ga 30281
www.lockdownpublications.com

Lock Down Publications
Like our page on Facebook: Lock Down Publications @
www.facebook.com/lockdownpublications.ldp
Book interior design by: **Shawn Walker**
Edited by: **Jill Alicea**

Stay Connected with Us!

Text **LOCKDOWN** to 22828 to stay up-to-date with new releases, sneak peaks, contests and more…

Thank you!

Submission Guideline.

Submit the first three chapters of your completed manuscript to ldpsubmissions@gmail.com, subject line: Your book's title. The manuscript must be in a .doc file and sent as an attachment. Document should be in Times New Roman, double spaced and in size 12 font. Also, provide your synopsis and full contact information. If sending multiple submissions, they must each be in a separate email.

Have a story but no way to send it electronically? You can still submit to LDP/Ca$h Presents. Send in the first three chapters, written or typed, of your completed manuscript to:

LDP: Submissions Dept
P.O. Box 944
Stockbridge, Ga 30281

DO NOT send original manuscript. Must be a duplicate.

Provide your synopsis and a cover letter containing your full contact information.

Thanks for considering LDP and Ca$h Presents.

Dedication

This book is dedicated to the memory of Kristie Fluker, a devout reader who with her support managed to touch the lives of too many urban authors to name.
Rest easy, Queen.

Acknowledgements

Thank you, God, for blessing me with the talent and time to be able to pen these novels.

I could not do this without my devout readers. Thank you all so much for the support. I'll name the ones I know, and much love to the rest.

Sharlene Smith, Mykia Hester, Nik Nicole, Cree Owens, Amy Withers, Carmelyn Braddock, Jillian Hathorn, Latasha Oliver, Dawn Avery, Nikolai Konstantin, Doris Beans, Lindsey Porter, Stephanie McLendon, Tangie Bryant, Pam Williams, Yaya Knight, Crystal Edwards, Karlton and Tori Benson, Schawanna Morris, Janiece Boyce, Angella Watkins, and Ava Moten.

If I missed you, please know that you are just as appreciated. Hope you all enjoy the read! Much more on the way!

King Rio

Prologue
Chicago, Illinois
February 15th, 2016
2:45 P.M.

Rell's laugh was not as sincere as it seemed.

His eyes were on the rearview mirror of his rented Mercedes Benz as he sat in the driver's seat smoking a Backwoods cigarillo full of OG Kush, and his hand was on the 30-shot clip that protruded out from the bottom of the Glock pistol on his lap.

Johnny B was in the backseat behind Rell. Jah, Rell's seventeen-year-old brother, was next to Rell in the passenger seat. They were laughing about the murder of an enemy, a hit that Rell had just handed Johnny B $10,000 for handling.

"We hit him up good, too," Johnny B was saying. "Caught his ass in traffic and let him have it. On Neal. Nigga didn't know what hit him. I had the K. Gave him the whole fifty out that muthafucka. I bumped into that nigga Zo coming out the store, but the law was parked right across the street. Next time I run into him, it's curtains."

Rell let out a chuckle and nodded his head. He looked out Jah's window at the group of young gang members who were standing on Shanita Lewis's front porch, then he moved his eyes up the street to his mother's house.

They were parked next to the boarded up Henson Elementary School on 13th and Avers Avenue, on the block where Rell and Jah were both born and raised. Across the street from the school stood a block-long strip of three-story homes. The one their mother, Maria, lived in had recently been shot up by a young guy named Zo, which was one of the dozen or so reasons that they were after him.

Rell and Jah had on black hoodies and sweatpants, and both of them had their hoods on their heads. Jah, dark and slim and permanently mean-faced, had a Mac-10 submachine gun on his lap. Although he was the younger brother, he was also the more violent. Rell was lighter in complexion and bulkier in muscle, but he and Jah looked remarkably similar in the face. They were both longtime members of the Traveler Vice Lords, a street gang that dominated a vast majority of the Lawndale neighborhood, as well as several other neighborhoods across the city. For years, Rell and Jah had been just as regular as the guys who were now standing on Shanita's front porch, but ever since they had inherited a combined $2.3 million from their father following his untimely death, they had essentially become the leaders of their gang, even though Rell and Jah had hardly spent any of the money.

Johnny B suggested that they get out and head inside Shanita's place. They were celebrating "D-Day", in memory of their fellow gang member D-Lo who had been killed in a shootout this past December.

Rell had Johnny B grab the bag of liquor off the backseat as he pushed open his door. Inside it were five bottles of Remy Martin VSOP, a drink that had been popularized within the squad by none other than D-Lo himself.

There was a small amount of snow falling from the clear blue sky. The only people outside were the guys and girls on Shanita's porch and a mailman down the street.

As Rell was walking up onto the porch, shaking hands with the guys, he noticed that Ciara, an ex-girlfriend of his, was standing among them. She was short and pretty-faced, a petite little lady who had broken his heart when she moved away to Kansas when they were both just sixteen.

"Ciara?" he said, surprised. She reached out to him for a hug, and he wrapped her up tight. "When you come back from Kansas?"

"Last week." She pulled back, studying him with the brightest of smiles. She had on a black bubble coat over blue jeans and furry black boots. "Just staying here for a few months with my auntie Shanita. Gotta get my shit back together. A bitch can't find a job out there in Kansas, and this fuck nigga I was messing with stole all my stuff on some dope fiend shit. Had to get out of there."

"Come on, we'll talk in here." He opened the door and let her walk in ahead of him.

He immediately noticed that she was no longer "Lil Booty Cee Cee", as the whole neighborhood had once called her.

"Yeah," she went on as they made it to the living room sofa, "I'll be good in no time. You know my hustle game is strong. My cousin Debra been doing the card-cracking and the tax scheme. I'm about to fuck with her on that. Should have about twenty grand by the end of the month. Waiting on the tax money to hit the cards, then I'm gone."

"Damn, you just got here. We miss your lil crazy ass," Rell said, grinning.

Ciara sucked her teeth and rolled her eyes. "Boy, please. I heard you proposed to that lil thot bitch Tamera. You thought I didn't know, huh? And I heard you proposed with a ring worth more than that Benz you got outside. You done came up and ain't even reached out to me. I should cuss your ass out."

Rell laughed. The ring she was referring to was the nine-carat engagement ring he'd proposed to his girlfriend Tamera with. It had been left to him by his father's wife, who had died in the same car accident that had taken his father's life. The ring was worth $100,000. It was the kind of ring that looked like it belonged on the finger of a Hollywood housewife. He remembered gawking at it the first time he'd seen it, and now he still could not believe that it was on his girlfriend's finger.

"Don't cuss me out. Damn." He smiled, biting down on the center of his lower lip.

He wanted so badly to take Ciara to the bedroom he still had at his mom's house and get a taste of what he'd been missing since she'd left. The temptation was real, but his love for Tamera was realer.

"It's all good. I'm straight. You know I'm straight." Ciara got up and put a hand on her hip. She sucked her teeth as she looked down at him. "Want me to make you a plate? My auntie cooked. She got some hot wings and some other shit."

"I don't know if I can trust you to make me a plate. You sounded a little too—"

"Great, never mind then," Ciara said, cutting him off mid-sentence and storming out of the living room.

"Yeah, make me one," Rell shouted after her with a chuckle.

"Too damn late for that," she shouted back.

Seated on the arm of the sofa across the room from Rell, Jah stared at his big brother and shook his head.

"Nigga, we just proposed to our girls yesterday and look at you. Already fuckin' up."

"Shut the fuck up, nigga," Rell said.

He wasn't surprised when Ciara returned to the living room with a plate for him. Jah cracked open the Remy and started filling up everyone's cups. Johnny B rolled two blunts and passed them around, and soon they were sitting beneath a heavy pall of Kush smoke.

Rell ate in silence, scrolling through Facebook on his iPhone with his free hand. Tamera was tagging him in all kinds of posts and her sister Tirzah — Jah's fiancée— had also

12

tagged him in a picture of Tamera sporting the ring. Everyone was congratulating them on their engagements. His cousin Tara had posted on his page demanding that he call her as soon as possible.

He went to her name in his phone contacts and was just about to dial the number when Capone, a fifteen-year-old member of the gang with dreadlocks that were longer than Johnny B's, rushed into the living room holding an AK-47 assault rifle.

"Just saw one of them niggas off 15th and Spaulding, bruh. One of Zo's lil homies. He down the street at Erica's house. Just walked in. Think he one of the niggas who work for Zo. Wanna send him a message?"

Erica was yet another one of Rell's exes. She was probably the easiest lay in the hood. Just about everyone had fucked her, or at least gotten their dicks sucked by her. He figured Zo's guy was just there to get his turn.

Rell set aside his empty plate and stood up. He was going to think over the idea of attacking Zo's worker until Jah got up and headed toward the front door with his Mac-10 in hand.

Without a second thought, Rell took the Glock out of his hoodie's belly pocket and followed his brother outside.

King Rio

Chapter 1

His name was James Ellis, and he was only at Erica's house because he'd heard how good her head game was and he wanted to experience it for himself. Zo had told him that Erica could make a nigga cum in less than five minutes. James had never shot off that quickly from getting top, and he hoped Zo's words were true.

She was wearing a tight little pair of shorts and a tee shirt when she opened the door. She rushed him in and slammed the door shut.

"Cold as fuck out there, boy. You gon' let all my damn heat out," she said, rubbing her arms. She went to the dining room, took a sweatshirt off the back of a chair, and put it on.

James wondered if her legs were cold.

"The hell you knocking on my door for anyway? If it's about that forty dollars I owe Zo, tell him he can kiss my ass 'cause I ain't got it til the first. Ol' tight-ass nigga. Got all that money and wanna hound a bitch about forty damn dollars. You the second nigga he done sent over here. Shit. Petty ass."

James smiled happily and raised the blunt he'd rolled before coming over. "I ain't come over here for no money for Zo. I just came to chill and smoke. It's cold and I gotta walk all the way back over to 15th and Christiana. Just wanted to warm up a little and kick it, smoke this loud with you. Calm down, lil lady. Ain't nobody hounding you about no forty bucks. Fuck I look like?"

Erica rolled her eyes and went to the kitchen. James gazed at her jiggling butt cheeks with a smirk on his ugly black face. He knew that more than likely he would never be able to get the kind of girl he wanted, but girls like Erica were his specialty. He had a ton of jokes that hardly ever failed to loosen up the easy ones like her. He was determined to get his dick sucked today. Zo said that all he had to do was get her high, get next to her, and pull his dick out.

He hoped Zo was right.

There was no sofa, just an air mattress on the dirty gray carpet and a beanbag in the corner. A small TV sat atop an upside down crate. An Adam Sandler movie was playing. The volume was turned up full blast. A bowl full of chicken bones sat next to the mattress. A vacuum cleaner stood like a soldier in the nearly empty closet next to the front door.

James took off his jacket and threw it on the vacuum cleaner before easing down onto the mattress. He inspected it and decided that it was sanitary enough to lie down on.

He let out a sigh as he fell back on his elbows and took the big gun off his hip. It was a .357 Glock that he'd gotten from Zo after Roddy, Zo's younger brother, was shot and killed yesterday morning.

Although no one had told the police, everybody knew that Jah had killed Roddy. It was only a matter of time before Jah got what was coming to him, and James was strapped and ready for it. Zo had $30,000 on Jah's head. James needed that money more than anything. He needed a car and his own apartment. The $400-$500 he made every day he worked for Zo was good money, but he had only worked five days so far this month, and that money had gone to clothes, shoes, his weed habit, and helping out his mom with the bills. He only had $400 and some change leftover, and now the block was too hot to hustle on so there would be no more money for a few days at least. The police wanted answers. Not only for Roddy's murder but also for Kendrick, Stain, Jamie, Webb, PJ, and all the other men who'd been recently shot dead in the neighborhood.

Erica was wiping her nose when she came back from the kitchen.

"Just snorted my last damn line. You got some coke?" she asked.

James shook his head no and raised the blunt. "I got this, though."

She plopped down on the mattress facing him, still rubbing her nose, her eyes as wide as saucers. He cast a blatant stare at the print of her pussy in the shorts.

"Unless you got the money to pay for it," she said, picking up a lighter from beside the bowl of chicken bones, "don't even look at it."

"Shit, how much I need?"

"A hundred."

"I got this blunt and a sawbuck."

A sawbuck meant ten dollars.

She sucked her teeth and snatched the blunt from him. As she lit it, her eyes wandered over to his gun.

"That big dumb-ass gun," she commented. "Yo' lil ass. Fuck around and break yo' arm shooting that damn thing."

"I ain't worried about it." James had the deep, gravelly voice of his father. "Long's it break a fuck nigga in half, it did its job."

"You know Jah's momma lives right down the street. I wouldn't be over here if I was you. I heard about the lil beef y'all got with Jah. That lil nigga ain't for none. If he see you over here, he gon' get to—"

"What? He gon' get to what? I got bullets like he got bullets. That tough shit don't move me. I'm on his ass when I see him, anyway. Shit, I hope I do run across that nigga. I just walked right past his momma house. Fuck that nigga."

"Yeah, a'ight. I'm just letting you know. I used to fuck with Rell. He was a monster his damn self, but I promise you that Jah is a hundred times worse. That lil nigga got like twenty bodies, and I ain't even exaggerating. You better ask around."

James gave Erica a look that made her shut up. She hit the blunt a couple of times and passed it to him. His eyes went back to her pussy as she leaned her head back and blew a line of smoke at the ceiling fan.

Her warning made him feel a bit uneasy. He got up and went to the window and fingered down the blinds.

There was nothing outside but a bunch of cars and trucks parked along the street and a mailman who was just leaving Erica's porch.

"Look at you," she said. "Tough ass. All scared and shit."

"I ain't scared of no nigga," James replied, but he was lying. Suddenly he found himself rethinking his decision to walk over here alone.

"You ain't gotta be scared, boy. They don't even be over here no more. They got all that money from Big Man dying and moved out of they momma's house. I don't know where they live now."

"I know." James sat back down on the mattress. "They got that house on Trumbull. Where ol' girl got hit up yesterday."

"Damn, that's right! Jah's baby momma! Felicia! Damn." Erica shook her head. "I heard she got shot through the damn door. Shot up real bad."

James grinned. Zo had shot Felicia after Jah killed Roddy. He'd told James all about it early this morning. James wasn't into hurting women, but he felt that he would have done the same thing had someone killed his brother. Kill mine, I'll kill yours, was his philosophy in that matter.

He finished smoking the blunt with Erica and then sat there next to her for a couple of minutes, watching the movie, but not really watching it at all. He was thinking about getting his dick sucked.

He took a deep breath as he whipped it out and started stroking it. For a moment, Erica acted like she didn't even notice what he was doing.

Then, just as Zo had predicted, she leaned forward and kissed the head of his dick before she took it into her mouth.

King Rio

Chapter 2

"Wanna kick the door in?" Jah asked.

Rell shook his head no. They were in the gangway next to the house where Erica lived — him, Jah, Capone, and Johnny B.

"Whatever we do," Johnny B said, "we need to hurry the fuck up. I'm not about to get caught out here with this choppa. Already got two bodies on this mu'fucka. Law run up on us while I got this on me, they gon' get it, on Neal."

"Just chill, bruh." Rell was thinking. He didn't want to try kicking in the door. Zo's guy could be strapped. What if he opened fire on them as soon as they kicked the door? Rell wasn't trying to be laid out like Felicia from catching shots through a door. Felicia was in critical condition at Northwestern Memorial Hospital. That was a condition that Rell wanted to avoid.

"I'll knock on the door," Capone suggested. "Dude don't even know me like that. I'll knock on the door and chop his ass down as soon as he answers."

Rell shook his head no again. He thought of his soon-to-be wife and wished that he could be making sweet love to her instead of standing here in the cold, plotting a murder. He was a millionaire now. What in the hell was he doing?

That's when it hit him.

He had over a million dollars in the bank, and almost $15,000 in hundred-dollar bills in his pocket. Jah had the same amount of money in the bank, give or take a few grand.

Neither of them belonged here.

Rell turned to Johnny B. "Why don't you and Capone just handle this? I'll give you another five racks. Fuck it. Me and lil bruh got too much bread now. We ain't supposed to be on this shit. Y'all need us out here to take care of shit if any of y'all get jammed up."

Capone said, "You right, big homie. Shit, gimme five racks and I'll do it all by myself. I don't need no help. Bruh just got down on ol' boy Kendrick for you. Lemme handle this one."

Rell could not hold back the smile. He patted Capone on the shoulder, and then jogged back to the alley with Jah and Johnny B.

They ran down to Shanita's backyard and went in through the back door. All eyes fell on them as they made it to the living room where everyone was seated.

"What happened?" Ciara asked.

"Nothing." Rell grabbed two of the unopened Remy bottles and said his goodbyes. He was going to sit in the Benz and wait for Capone to take care of business.

"Wait." Ciara caught up with him just as he made it out to the front porch. "You didn't take my number down. Or give me yours."

Rell hesitated. Part of him wanted to give her his number, but the other part of him loved Tamera too much to make such a disloyal move.

"I can't do it. I'll see you around," he said, and left her standing there in the doorway as he jogged down the stairs and across the street to his car, looking over to his left to see if the guy had left Erica's home.

Jah got in the car with him, and Johnny B stayed on Shanita's porch.

Everyone focused on the house where Erica lived and waited on her little friend to make his exit.

"Ciara done got thick, bruh," Jah said. "I know you noticed that shit. Her lil ass ain't never been that fat. Keep it a hundred: you wanted to smash, didn't you? I know I did."

"I ain't on that."

A moment of silence followed.

"Lil homie ain't never caught no bodies," Jah said finally. "Hope he don't freeze up."

"He ain't gon' freeze up. That five racks gon' thaw out whatever ice he got in him."

"You never know, bruh. It's a bitch to whack a nigga for the first time. I still remember my first body. Shit was crazy."

The memory of Rell's first homicide floated to the surface of his own memory as he began counting out the $5,000 for Capone. It had been a gang hit. A member of the Mafia Insane Vice Lords had snitched on a botched robbery that had turned into a murder, and when he was released from jail, the order was passed down to Rell to whack the snitch before he could testify in open court. Rell had kicked it with the snitch for nearly a week before finally shooting the rat in the head while they were stopped at a red light. He still remembered vividly the sound of the gunshot and the sight of the boy's brains splattering all over the driver door. He had feared that the boy's foot might stomp down on the gas pedal, so he'd thrown the car in park just as he pulled the trigger. It turned out he was right. The engine had revved loudly as he ran off into the night. It was a sound that he would never forget.

"Once we take care of Zo and Tremaine, I'm out of here, big bruh. On D-Lo's grave. I'm out this bitch. Me and Tirzah gon' move out the hood. We can stay in the city, but I'm going somewhere nice. This shit ain't what's up. I should've listened to you from the jump. If I would've listened, that hoe-ass nigga wouldn't have been able to rape baby."

Yesterday, Jah's fiancée had been raped by a high-ranking Unknown Vice Lord named Tremaine. Their cousin Tara had told them where Tremaine was staying, and they'd been driving past the house all morning, but had yet to spot him.

"What's even more fucked up," Jah continued, "is that Johnny B done got into it with the GDs on Instagram for some shit he said on somebody's page, so now we gotta be on alert for that shit, too. You know how they comin'. We gotta be ready to lay them down, lay Tremaine down, lay Zo down — this shit ain't gon' end, big bruh. It's like we stuck in this shit."

Rell understood exactly what Jah meant. Things were getting hectic in the streets. There were so many bodies dropping, and with them both now engaged, it seemed like all the drama was popping off at the wrong time.

Just then, his eyes widened as Erica's front door opened. A dark-skinned boy stuck his head out and looked both ways before stepping out onto the porch. Rell and Jah sank down in their seats.

Then it happened.

Capone ran out from beside the house with his AK-47 raised just as the boy made it to the stairs. Fire leapt out of the assault rifle's barrel, and the boy collapsed on the porch. Capone ran up on the porch and kept firing, then took off running back into the gangway.

Hardly two minutes passed before Capone came strolling casually out of Shanita's front door, breathing hard, smiling from ear to ear, and no longer toting the assault rifle.

He got in the backseat, and Rell sped off.

Chapter 3

Tamera and Tirzah Lyon were both hot and sweaty and in serious pain.

They were doing squats in the living room of Rell's living room. They had moved the glass-top coffee table aside in preparation for their workout. Both of them wore tight gray Nike leggings and sports bras. Tirzah's long braids were pulled back in a ponytail, and Tamera's fresh bob was wrapped up in a white Gucci headscarf. They were watching a YouTube video on the 65-inch television of a woman instructing them how to tighten up their abs while at the same time getting their derrières right. Today was their first day working out, and it was killing them.

"It's break time, bitch," Tirzah said as she dropped to the floor and lay flat on her back, chest rising and falling rapidly.

Tamera was all too glad to lay up next to her sister at that very moment. Her entire body was weak. Her sports bra and leggings were heavily saturated with sweat.

"Bitch, if Jah doesn't massage my body when he gets in here, the engagement's off," Tirzah said.

"Tell me about it."

"You got me doing these white people exercises. Black folks don't do this kinda shit. Ugh. I fucking hate you so much right now, Tamera. I could bust your head."

"And you could lay in the same hospital room your man's baby's momma is stretched out in," Tamera shot back.

They laughed at this. Tamera reached over and picked up her bottle of ice-cold water. She sat up and drank it thirstily.

"I can't wait until Jah turns eighteen." Tirzah got to drinking her own bottle of water. "I can't get married to no damn seventeen-year-old. Fuck around and have me on Jerry Springer."

"No, Maury. On the show where it's an old-ass woman married to a teenager."

"A'ight now, hoe. I ain't that old." Tirzah cut a tight glance at her younger sister. She was light-skinned and much thicker than Tamera. Neither of them really needed the workout. Their bodies were perfect. Their stomachs were tight and their asses were the talk of the neighborhood. They had only exercised because of their upcoming weddings.

"I'm about to get in the shower," Tirzah said, getting up. "Call Tara and see what she's doing for the night. Tell her to come over and play Spades with us or something. I ain't tryna be sitting in here bored tonight."

Tamera nodded her head while still lying flat on her back, trying to catch her breath. She thought about the bullet holes in the front door from Felicia being shot yesterday and suddenly became fearful of it happening again, which gave her the energy to get up and go to the soft leather sofa where her Michael Kors bag was sitting. She had a subcompact Glock handgun in the bag.

She dialed Tara's number on her iPhone 6S and turned to stretch out on the sofa as the phone rang.

"Hey, girl," Tara answered.

"Bitch, I am dead tired, you hear me? Me and Tirz just did the craziest workout."

"Workout? What are y'all working out for? You hoes that bored sitting in the house?"

"No, boo. I gotta be right for my wedding. I want that dress to fit perfectly on me. I want your lil cousin to be looking at me and only me for the rest of his life."

"You ain't gotta worry about that. Rell's a real nigga. Trust me, after him going through what he went through with Erica, that nigga is going to love you to death. He's a good man, Tamera. I mean that. I know my cousin like the back of my hand. He might be a savage to these niggas in the streets, but he has the sweetest heart. He'll bend over backwards for the people he loves and won't expect a single thing in return. You got a good one, girl. Once he's with you, he's with you."

"I know." Tamera sighed, rubbing a hand across her aching abdomen. "He's the apple of my eye, whatever the hell that means. I love that boy so much." She raised her left hand and stared at the engagement ring. "He made my dreams come true."

"What y'all on tonight?"

"That's what I was calling you for."

"Me and K just came back from visiting his brother. You remember Buck off Trumbull?"

"Who doesn't know Buck's crazy ass?"

"Yeah, you know they used to live in that same house y'all stay in. But anyway, we just left the prison. On our way home now. Gotta take Kayshawn to the dentist and then our day is pretty much clear."

"Spades?"

"I'm down." Tara asked her husband K if he wanted to come over and play Spades and then got back on the phone. "He's with it. About what time?"

Tamera glanced at the rose gold Michael Kors watch Rell had bought her a few weeks ago. "It's 3:30 now. Is seven cool?"

"Yep. Perfect. Do I need to bring drinks?"

"Is our president Black?"

Tamera cracked up laughing. "Okay, girl. Bring some Remy if you can. You know it's D-Lo's birthday. Everybody's drinking Remy. I'll pay you for it when you get here."

"Okay, I got you. I still have some money from what Rell and that pussy nigga Tremaine gave K yesterday. You don't have to pay me back."

"No, I insist. We're straight. Not trying to rub it in your face or anything but I don't need it and I'd rather help you — somebody I know, somebody who's related to my fiancé — than to help anyone else. You deserve it. Most of these hoes around here ain't gonna ever get married. I think you might have influenced Rell and Jah in a good way, you know what I mean? I don't know. Maybe I'm just thinking too much."

"No, I understand. Trust me when I say that I wanted a good man for a long time before K came along, and I'm so grateful. I'm a bitch from the hood just like you, and it's almost impossible to find a loyal man out here nowadays. I'm so glad that my lil Cuz can be that for you."

"Aww, thanks, cousin." Tamera teared up. Looking at the ring and hearing Tara's kind words was too much to bear. She sniffled once and thumbed away the tears. "You're making me cry, bitch. Please don't do that to me."

Tara laughed, and Tamera's laugh ensued. She inhaled sharply and said, "I love you, girl. Come on over. I'll cook the pizzas we have in the freezer. We still got a few ounces of Kush to smoke. It'll be a good night."

"Okay, I'll call when I'm on the way over," Tara said before hanging up.

Tamera lay silently on the sofa after the call, thinking. She loved her man more than she'd ever loved anyone in her entire life. Rell was everything she'd ever dreamed of and more. He was handsome, intelligent, loyal, loving, romantic, selfless, and everything else she'd ever wanted in a man. She thought back to the day when she'd first laid eyes on him. He had knocked on the door of the apartment she'd shared with Tirzah and smiled his wonderful smile when she opened the door. Sure, he had been coming to collect the rent money, but that had not deterred Tamera from falling in love with him at first sight. Ever since that day, the two of them had gone through hell and back in the streets, but it had only served to strengthen their love for one other. Now that they were engaged, Tamera was determined to be the best woman she could be to him. She'd made a promise to herself that she would be the best wife he could have ever dreamed of having.

She got up, legs weak, and went to the bathroom to use the toilet. Tirzah was soaking in the tub.

"Bitch, you better not be taking a shit," Tirzah said as Tamera sat down on the stool.

"If I'm not mistaken, you and Jah live upstairs," Tamera retorted. "This is my bathroom. And you better clean out that tub so I can get in it next. Hoe."

Tamera emptied her bowels and pissed and flushed in a hurry. She didn't need Tirzah getting on her about it. Tirz was known to go hard with the jokes. She cleaned herself and then flushed again.

"Bitch, you ain't slick. I smell that nasty shit." Tirzah missed nothing, even with her eyes closed.

"You don't smell a damn thing, so quit it."

"You'sa damn lie. I smell shit. Either you just took a dump, or you need to get checked out."

"Shut up talking to me, Tirzah." Tamera went to the sink and washed her hands. "I just got off the phone with Tara. They're coming over to play Spades with us tonight. I told her to bring some Remy."

"That's cool. I like Tara. She's a real bitch." Tirzah paused; then, "What do you think about what's going on between Zo and Jah?"

"That nigga Zo kidnapped you. Fuck you mean? I think his ass needs to be dead. No ifs, ands, or buts about it."

"I agree with you a hundred percent. But with all that's been happening, don't you think we should maybe take a vacation for a few weeks or so? To get away from this bullshit for a while?"

"I don't see the sense in running from it, Tirzah. Chicago is our home. Fuck leaving. Especially if it's because of some bitch niggas. I'm not backing down from nobody, and I don't want my man backing down. Rell and Jah will handle that shit, and if they so happen to get jammed up, then I guess we'll be prison wives. I'm rolling until the wheels fall off."

"I am, too. I'm just saying, we have to be smart. Look at Kanye West and Chief Keef. Their asses are way out in California. Maybe we need to leave. I mean, our men have money now. They're no longer your average trap niggas. We gotta adjust to the situation."

Tamera went back to the toilet, dropped the seat, and sat down. Tirzah opened her eyes and looked over at Tamera.

"Funky-booty ass," Tirzah said.

Tamera flipped a middle finger. "Fuck you."

Tirzah laughed and switched subjects. "Can't believe I'm twenty-six with a fiancé who's seventeen. I feel like a child molester."

"It's because you are a child molester."

"Shit, if you saw that dick, you'd know he wasn't as much of a child as you think he is."

"I don't wanna hear about some underage boy's dick. Especially not from my thirty-year-old sister."

"Bitch, I ain't thirty." Tirzah threw some bubbles from her bath at Tamera. "Believe me, I would not be fucking with that lil boy if he wasn't already so grown mentally. He's more of an OG than most of these old niggas. He got the whole hood scared. I'm proud to call him my bae. You know that ain't nobody around here got niggas shook the way Jah does."

Tamera nodded her head in agreement. Tirzah was right. Jahlil Owens had the whole neighborhood shook. Everywhere they went, people talked about him like a legend, and he wasn't even legally grown yet. To Tamera it felt good having him as a brother-in-law, though it was strange to think that if he had a child with Tirzah his kid would be both her nephew and nephew-in-law, or however it went.

"It's kinda weird that we're marrying brothers, ain't it?"

"Yeah," Tirzah said. "And that they're marrying sisters."

"Love is love, though."

"It most definitely is."

"Have you thought about what you and Jah are gonna name your kids?"

"Jasmine if it's a daughter," Tirzah said quickly, obviously having already considered it. "Jahlil Junior if it's a boy. You? And you better not say no stupid shit like Sharonikalesque or some shit."

Tamera laughed. "Bitch, I'm ghetto, but not that damn ghetto. I was thinking Cassandra, after Momma. Or Anthony if it's a boy. I don't know why, but I like Anthony."

"It's a cool name. Regular."

"Yeah." Tamera became thoughtful. "We should get married together. On the same day, or even at the same time. We might as well, since we're all brothers and sisters. That way the family won't have to do it twice. We'd save money."

"I don't know, bitch. Depends on what kind of wedding y'all trying to have. I'm not with the bullshit. If it's some weird shit, I'm cool."

Tamera turned and searched for something to throw at Tirzah. She decided on a bar of Dial soap and flung it at Tirzah's head. It clunked Tirzah right on the ear and she shouted, "Bitch!"

Tamera hopped up and ran out of the bathroom while Tirzah reached in the water to find the bar of soap.

Just as she made it back to the living room, Rell and Jah came walking in the door.

Rell looked at Tamera's leggings and said, "Aw, yeah. You know what time it is. To the bedroom."

Chapter 4

She took a bath first.

Rell was waiting in bed for her when she walked in the bedroom wearing a pair of white sweatpants and a tee shirt. He kept glancing from his smartphone to her as she put on some deodorant and then climbed in bed next to him. He set his gun and the iPhone on his nightstand and plugged in the charger.

"Why you leave the door open?" he asked as he took off his hoodie.

"Didn't know there was a rule saying that I had to close it whenever I came in here."

"Well, it is."

"'There is', you mean?"

"I mean what I said, goofy-ass girl. Gimme a kiss." He puckered his lips and she pressed hers against his. She had the kind of lips that were meant for kissing: thick, full lips that were always juicy with gloss and just waiting to be sucked on.

When their lips separated, she said, "What happened with Tremaine? Y'all find him?"

Rell shook his head no. "We drove through there, but didn't see him. We gon' slide back down on his block later to see if that Jag out there. That's all we're waiting for. Soon's we see that mu'fucka, I'ma wait until he comes out and...you know."

"Yeah," Tamera said in a defeated tone. "I know. You pay Johnny B?"

He nodded his head yes. "Had to get him out the way. He say he bumped into Zo at the store on Drake. Said if twelve wasn't parked across the street, he would've whacked him."

"Yesterday was the best day ever, Rell. I mean that. You're the best." She looked at the engagement ring on her finger. "Oh, my God, everybody on Facebook's been commenting on it. It got over a thousand likes and like a hundred shares. I tagged you in it."

Rell shrugged his shoulders dismissively. He didn't care much for Facebook. All the guys were hooked on Instagram and Twitter.

"Don't shrug your shoulders, you asshole." She put a fingertip on his jaw and gave it a light shove. "This ring means everything to me, Rell. It's the most beautiful ring in the fucking world, and it's mine. Don't just shrug it off. I'm sensitive about that kinda shit. Oh, and since we're talking about Facebook—"

"I'm not talking about Facebook."

"Whatever. You know what I mean. While I'm on the subject of Facebook, I'ma need you to, ummm, unfriend some hoes. Might need to block a couple of 'em, too."

Rell chuckled and pecked his lips on the tip of her nose.

"Lemme see your phone and I'll do it for you." Tamera was persistent.

"Hell nah. You crazy? I got so many female friends on there. Most 'em I ain't talked to in forever."

"That's not the point. Hoes will be hoes. I don't want 'em on your page. And by the way, if you got any exes on your page, please let me know right the fuck now. I'm not trying to be friends with none of those nasty-ass girls."

"You take Facebook way too seriously. Don't start with that shit. Fuck Facebook. Worry about what's going on in here." He slapped a hand onto her left butt cheek and gave it a firm squeeze. Biting his bottom lip, he regarded her with an expression of pure lust. He knew that she understood what the look meant. She'd seen it far too many times not to know.

Looking at her now, he realized why he'd turned Ciara down a short while ago. Sure, Ciara was stunning, but she had nothing on Tamera. Tamera possessed the face of a model, like the *Real Housewives of Atlanta's* Cynthia Bailey, and she had a body like Porsha Williams. She was the most beautiful, curvaceous woman Rell had ever been with, and she was a fool if she thought he was going to let some Facebook women get in the way of what they had going.

"You're a smooth talker, Rell. Just don't let me find out you've been talking to one of those bitches. I'm so serious." She reached a hand in his pants and squeezed his dick just as tightly as he was squeezing on her ass. "Play with me if you wanna. You'll lose it."

"Lose what? My dick?"

"Damn right."

"Damn wrong."

"Snip, snip, snip."

"You trying to get beat up the day after Valentine's Day?"

"You ain't gon' beat up nothing but this pussy with that tongue of yours." She mounted him, and he put his hands on her bountiful ass. "Guess I should've shut the door, huh?" She snickered.

"Told you."

"I wanna get married here in Chicago this summer. Somewhere like the Trump Tower. People get married there all the time. And there's a lot of room. We can invite everybody. Shouldn't cost us no more than fifty grand."

"I told you I'm not spending that much money on—"

"It's my day, Rell. The only day that's meant for me. Don't spoil my day. Fifty thousand dollars is nothing. As a matter of fact, you need to get that dope out of here, anyway. I know we can get at least eighty or ninety grand. That's a kilo and a half of heroin."

They had fifty-three ounces of heroin stashed away in a suitcase in their closet. Rell had yet to tell Jah about it. The heroin had come from the suitcase full of cash Tamera had taken from the girl who set up Tirzah to get kidnapped back in December. She had split the cash — a few thousand shy of $200,000 — with Rell, Jah, and Tirzah, but the dope had yet to be touched.

The reason Rell had not touched the heroin was because he was leery of being caught with it. He'd spent enough time in prison, and he wasn't trying to go back. But Tamera had a point. The dope had to go. Yesterday their house had been surrounded by police following the shooting that landed Felicia in the hospital. With so much drama going on in the streets, it wasn't good to have so much dope in the house. He'd get a life sentence if the house was ever raided.

"I'm about to start dumping it on Johnny B and Lil Larry," he said. "I'll weigh up two ounces and charge 'em $75 a gram. We gotta take it somewhere else, too. I don't want it here."

"That makes two of us."

"That shit'll go so fast if it's good dope. You know how that boy sells."

"Seventy-five damn dollars for every gram," Tamera said, shaking her head in disbelief. "That's gonna be about a hundred thousand dollars for us at the end."

"Double if I step on it "

"You should definitely do that."

Rell laughed. "Nah. I ain't gon' be greedy. That'll get you caught up every time. The people in the house on Harding just moved out. We can stash the dope somewhere in there until we get another renter."

"We should move over there. Zo knows we live here, Rell. I'm not comfortable with that. He already shot through

36

our damn door. And you know he'll shoot up the house. If he did it to your mom's house, he'll definitely do it to yours."

"Nuh uh. I ain't moving nowhere. We can leave for a few weeks if you wanna, but I'm staying right where I'm at for now. He'll be gone just like Kendrick soon, anyway. Don't even worry about it. Jah got four of his lil guys watching this block and our house 24/7. If anybody pulls up we'll know it."

Tamera got quiet for a moment, staring down at him with a look of disagreement. She obviously was not feeling his position on the matter of their safety.

"Remember what you told me at the hotel yesterday?" she said finally.

"What?"

"You said you were going to do some things to make our lives better. In fact, you said we were going to move into a bigger house, get new cars — you said a lot of shit. Was that all for show? Were you just telling me what I wanted to hear? Because if we're gonna start off with lies, then—"

"Alright, alright, alright. You're right. We'll move. We'll go looking for a new spot tomorrow. Now, can you close the door and lock it and get naked? Damn."

A huge smile grew on Tamera's face as she hopped out of bed and went to the door. She was back two seconds later, kicking off her sweatpants as she leapt on top of him.

"I knew you'd see it my way," she said.

Rell could do nothing but laugh. His usual self would not have folded under any circumstances, but Tamera Lyon had him wrapped around her finger.

King Rio

Chapter 5

"Realest niggas in the game left
  Realest niggas in the game left
  Realest niggas in the game left
  As I look around, we the realest in the game left…"

The Jadakiss track that was throbbing from the speakers in the trunk of Zo's new-model Cadillac CTS had the block shaking as he turned the corner onto 18th and Millard to drop his girlfriend Zaniyah off at her aunt's house.

Zaniyah said something to him as he pulled over to the curb, but he couldn't hear what she said, so he lowered the music volume.

"What?"

"I said thanks, bae. For the clothes. I really appreciate it."

Zo had just taken her shopping with him downtown on Michigan Avenue. He'd only gone to get his mind off the loss of his baby brother and to get away from his sister Odella, who had yet to stop crying. She had two reasons to cry. Not only had she lost a brother, but her one-year-old daughter's father, Kendrick, had also been shot dead yesterday. Zo, too, had shed a fair amount of tears last night. He was already missing Roddy like crazy.

He turned off the engine, and he and Zaniyah sat in silence for a minute. It felt good having someone at his side at a time like this. He was at odds with Jah, the most ruthless young nigga in the neighborhood. He needed an extra set of eyes to keep watch, just in case he slipped up and missed seeing something that could cost him his life.

Zaniyah was looking beautiful in her tight pink jeans. Her boots, lips, and fingernails matched them, and there was also a bit of pink highlight in her curly black hair. The Gucci bag on her lap had cost Zo $2,200 alone. He couldn't believe he'd blown almost $70,000 on their shopping trip, but since he now had over $300,000 in drug money hidden away in his paternal grandmother's south side home, he didn't feel so bad about it. Most of it he'd spent on himself. He had on a black pair of red-bottomed Christian Louboutin sneakers, Balmain jeans of the same color with a black Gucci belt, a gray and black Balmain sweatshirt, and a gold Rolex watch. His dreadlocks were freshly oiled and hanging down over his face. And he had a 9 millimeter Glock with red laser sighting and a 50-round drum magazine on his lap.

"I know this might not be the best time to ask you this," Zaniyah said, "but did Roddy have life insurance? To cover the funeral expenses, I mean."

Zo shook his head, looking around. "I'ma take care of it, though. Shit, I can't believe Jah took my lil nigga from me. All this shit started 'cause E and Chris had the bright idea to rob Rell. I told them dumb-ass niggas it was a stupid idea. We didn't have no masks on or nothing. That was just dumb. Now E and Chris dead. My lil brotha gone. All I can think about is how dumb I was to go along with the shit in the first place. If I would've just kept my ass in the house, none of this shit would've happened."

"Yeah, and you would also still be broke as fuck. Come on, Zo. You know that everything happens for a reason. Don't blame yourself for none of this shit. There's nothing you can do to change the past. All you can do is make sure your future is straight, and the way it's looking, you pretty much got that covered. Your only real problem is those fuck boys on Trumbull. If they didn't have girlfriends I'd set them up for you so we can finally get the shit over."

Zo picked up his smartphone to answer an incoming call from Don Don, a fourteen-year-old member of the 4 Corner Hustlers who sold dope for him on 16th and Christiana.

"What's up?" Zo answered dryly.

"Got this bread for you. Need two more G packs. Almost sold out."

"A'ight, I'll be through in a minute."

"You hear about what just happened to James? Somebody clapped bruh down over there on D Block. You already know who it had to be."

Zo's mouth fell open at the news. "Is he dead?"

"Yup. Say they hit him with a choppa, got him covered in a sheet on Erica's front porch right now, joe. Man, shit is fucked up out here. We got our eyes on every car that drive through this bitch. Let a nigga try to slide on the Ana if they want to. They won't make it to the other end of this bitch."

Zo clenched his teeth together and shook his head. He couldn't believe it. Knowing that Erica lived on Jah's old block, he had warned James not to go over there without security, and apparently, James hadn't listened.

After ending the call Zo sat silently for almost a full minute, gritting his teeth, flaring his nostrils, and plotting on a way to get to Jah.

His eyes lit up when the idea hit him.

King Rio

Chapter 6

Looking down at the top of Rell's head as he sucked and tongued her clitoris, gripping her meaty thighs in his hands, Tamera could not hold in the loud moans that now had Tirzah yelling in from the hallway.

"Bitch, me and bae are going upstairs until you and Rell finish doing the nasty, because I am not trying to hear these loud-ass animal screams. Sound like a fucking...giraffe. Like a giraffe fucking a zebra. Bye, bitch."

Both Tamera and Rell laughed.

"How in the fuck does she know how a giraffe fucking a zebra sounds?" Rell asked as he rose to his knees and then lowered his juice-laden mouth to Tamera's for a kiss.

"Hell if I know." Tamera giggled. "That's no excuse for you to stop sucking on this pussy."

"I love you." He grinned.

"Nuh uh, that shit ain't gonna fly. You can put that bull-shit right back where you found it."

He lay on his back. "Come on. Sixty-nine. You gon' suck this dick at the same time if I can't stop sucking that pussy when I want to."

"I ain't got a problem with that," Tamera said.

She was all smiles. Although she would never blatantly say it to him, she actually loved sucking Rell's dick. She liked the feel of it in her mouth. She liked the taste of it. She liked when she took her mouth off it and saw the string of precum stretching from her lip to its head. And most of all, she liked the cum. Sometimes she let him plaster her face with it. Sometimes she let him blast off all over her tits. Sometimes he came in her pussy, and she always held it in, unwilling to miss an opportunity to have his baby. At other times, she let him cum in her mouth, and with him having such a large amount of se-men in those heavy balls of his, she often found it difficult to swallow his thick cum, but she'd done it three times in the past. Each time she had gagged and nearly vomited, but she had kept sucking him afterward. She wanted her man to be completely pleased with her sexual abilities so that he would never have to go in search of good loving somewhere else.

She got on top of him in the sixty-nine position and just about slammed her pussy down onto his mouth. He chuckled and immediately went back to eating her juicy nookie while she stroked his huge dick and spit on it.

He had one of those dicks that was too fat for its own good. His dick was thicker than her wrist, and it wasn't short, either. She sucked the head of it into her mouth and kneaded his balls at the same time. Then she started bobbing up and down, stopping every ten seconds or so to spit on it before sucking it back into her tightly sucking mouth. It was long enough that she could grip its base in one hand, hold his balls in the other, and still jam the head to the back of her throat every time she went down on it.

The feeling of his tongue on her pussy and his dick half-way down her throat put Tamera on cloud 9. Maybe cloud 100 was a better term, because she could not imagine a better feel-ing. He ate pussy like a champ. His tongue battered her clitoris as if it had in some way disrespected him.

An even louder moan escaped her throat as she came, and she shook and shivered and quivered as it happened, loosening her oral grip on his dick and just stroking it in her hands. His tongue delved into her pussy to suck up her juices.

She took her mouth off him and said, "Oh, my God, Rell. Shit."

He chuckled.

She moved to position her dripping nookie over his throbbing hard love stick and slowly guided it into her. She let out another moan.

"Yassssss," she said, laughing.

"Yeaaaah. It's Mr. Nasty time."

"Shut up, asshole."

He slapped her on the ass and pulled her down on his dick. She gasped as it filled her. She still had on her T-shirt, but that was all. Nothing else except for the socks on her feet.

She began riding his dick with her back to him, loving the feel of his hands rubbing down her back and all over her hips and ass. She put her head down and leaned forward on her fingertips. She did her signature move, slamming down on his dick so hard that her ass made slapping sounds every time she bounced down on him.

When she raised her head seconds later, she gazed at her reflection in the dresser mirror. She looked damn good, in her opinion.

"This what I'm talking 'bout, baby," Rell said, his hands on her waist. "Bounce it for me. Buss it open for a real nigga."

He grunted and endured the wild ride for about ten minutes before she turned around to face him.

Looking down at him and tracing her tongue across her upper lip, she clawed at his bulging pectoral muscles and went back to riding him.

"I love you, baby," he said.

"I love you...mmm...more," she replied.

His dick was so big that she wondered how she was able to take it all in. He slipped a hand under her T-shirt and massaged her breasts while his other hand held onto her thigh.

When she had to stop for a few seconds to catch her breath, she kissed his sexy lips and then whispered in his ear: "It's so big. Mmm. It hurts."

"You'll be okay." He slapped his hands on her ass. "I got faith in you."

"I bet you do. Asshole."

"Keep calling me that and I'ma stick a finger in yours."

"Go ahead. I ain't tripping."

She wasn't sure if she'd really wanted him to do it, but once his finger was in there, she didn't mind. She went back to riding him, slowly at first, then speeding up as he slapped and squeezed her fluffy buttocks. The only items of clothing he had on were his socks and his boxers, the latter of which were way down at his ankles.

There were dozens of tattoos on his chest and abdomen. Gang signs, guns, bullets, hundred-dollar bills, RIPs, the Chicago Bulls mascot holding an assault rifle, and a money bag that was overflowing with cash. All the ink was spread so perfectly across his smooth brown skin and sharply defined musculature that Tamera found it hard to believe that he had gotten it done in prison and not by a professional tattoo artist. (It did not occur to her that a professional tattoo artist might have been in prison with him).

Taking in both his handsomeness and his oversized phallus proved to be too much for her.

She came again, and as it happened, Rell flipped her over onto her back, pushed her legs up, and pounded in and out of her as her vaginal walls contracted repeatedly in orgasm.

"Yeah...it got tighter," Rell said, smiling and nodding his head. "Wetter, too. I made you cum again already, huh? I got that dope dick."

The orgasm was too powerful; Tamera could not reply to his cocky remark. All she could do was gaze up at him with her mouth wide open until the overwhelming orgasm subsided.

Just as she was regaining her self-control, Rell buried his dick balls-deep in her and grunted as it twitched around inside her and filled her with semen. He sucked and kissed on the side of her neck until his dick went limp and then rolled over and lay next to her, turning his head to look at her and grinning broadly.

She put the palm of her hand on his face and gave it a shove. "Get the fuck out my face," she said with a laugh.

Rell laughed with her, pulling up his boxers and flexing his abdominal muscles to gawk at his incredible six-pack.

She took some time to catch her breath and then turned to face him. The silk pillowcase felt amazingly soft on her face. She planted a kiss on Rell's shoulder.

"There's something I need to tell you," she said.

He looked over at her. "Something like what?"

"I love you."

"Don't start with that crazy shit."

"It's not crazy. It's the truth. I love you so much. Way more than I've ever loved anybody. You've taken my heart. Don't fucking rip it to pieces, please and thank you."

He pinched her chin between his thumb and forefinger and brushed his lips over hers before pressing closer for a gentle kiss.

"I won't break your heart, baby," he said, sneaking a hand under her tee shirt to rub on her breasts. "I promise."

Tamera believed him.

King Rio

Chapter 7

"Girl, yo' daddy got me running around like a chicken with its head cut off, feeding you and changing your diapers and everything else, and his ass ain't even tried to come over and help. Young dummy, you know that? Mm-hmm. That's what your daddy is. He's a young dummy. Should've waited til he was older to have a baby."

Maria was walking to and from her kitchen, simultaneously warming up Dora's bottle of milk in a bowl of hot water in the sink, cooking herself two Polish sausages, and cleaning up Dora's toys and other things off her living room floor while Dora followed her around with a pacifier in her mouth and a half empty bag of barbecue Ruffles potato chips in her hand.

Maria kept looking out the window every time she came into the living room. She had heard the gunshots a few hours ago, and now there were CPD vehicles and policemen all over the street. A few of them were patting down three teenage boys in front of the school across the street. Several more were looking under cars and in bushes. But the majority of them were at the house where Erica lived down the street, snapping pictures of gun shells on the ground and the sheet covered corpse on the porch and talking to each other.

"This shit is getting out of control. It just don't make no sense. All this killing. If you live past the age of twenty these days, it's a miracle." Maria was talking to herself, as she sometimes did when she didn't have company. She sat down and blew out a sigh of relief. She needed a minute or two of rest before she got back up.

Dora stopped walking and stood at the other side of the coffee table, staring at her grandma with her eyebrows raised, smiling and holding up her bag of chips.

"The hell you looking at?" Maria said.

Dora giggled.

"I'ma bust your daddy's head if he don't pay me for all this damn babysitting."

"Da?"

"Yeah. Yo' damn 'Da' better pay me some 'ca' before his head get 'cra'. You understand that?"

Dora turned the bag of potato chips upside down and dumped them out. Some of the chips landed on the table, and the rest of them hit the floor.

"You lil..." Maria got up to slap Dora on the butt, and Dora must have sensed it, because she turned and took off running to Maria's bedroom.

"I'ma kick yo' lil ass you do this mess again, you hear me, Dora? A'ight now. I'll knock out a kid, too. Better quit testing my gangsta 'fore I show you how Grandma really get down."

Maria started picking up the potato chips, shaking her head and muttering more threats that were directed at Dora and Jah. She was a forty-one-year-old anesthesiologist at Northwestern Memorial Hospital. Last night, she had administered the anesthetics to Felicia Sanders, Dora's mother, during an intense four-hour surgery to repair the damage the bullets had done to Felicia's organs. Now she was operating on five hours of sleep, babysitting Felicia and Jah's evil little girl, and all she had was one cigarette left in her pack.

"Keep it up, Dora," she said. "They gon' have me on CNN for fucking up my own grandbaby. Don't know why you think it's a game."

Just as she collected the last chip and dropped it in the trash can in her dining room, someone knocked at the front door.

Instinctively, she reached down in her purse and pulled out her gun, a semiautomatic Glock that Rell had given her after her house was shot up a few months ago.

"Who is it?" she shouted, half expecting it to be a policeman asking questions about the shooting down the street but still cautious.

"It's Ciara. Shanita's niece."

"Rell's old girlfriend?"

"Yes, ma'am," Ciara replied cheerfully.

Maria went to the front window with her gun in hand and peeked out to make sure that it was really Ciara before she put the gun away and opened the door.

"Hey, Cee Cee!" Maria said, wearing the widest smile as she reached out to Ciara for a hug. "Girl, where the hell you been? Ain't seen you in years. Come on in and have a seat. I got some Polishes on the stove if you're hungry."

Ciara came in and sat down on the sofa, and Maria quickly shut and locked the door.

"No, I'm fine," Ciara said, her eyes roaming the pictures of Rell and Jah on the coffee table. "Just finished eating. Shanita cooked a bunch of food for D-Lo's party. You know today is his birthday."

Maria was shaking her head as she went to the kitchen and got Dora's bottle from beneath the hot water. She shook it up and squeezed a couple of drops on the back of her hand to see if it was too hot, then put it on the table and opened a bag of hot dog buns.

"I used to work with D-Lo's grandmother," Maria said, preparing her Polish sausage. "At the post office. This was back in the nineties. We didn't get along for shit, but sometimes we talked. I still remember the day she told me her daughter had just given birth to a baby boy, and now look. The lil boy's dead already. Damn shame. You know, it wasn't like this when I was a kid. When I was your age, we lived right off Ogden, and I can't remember ever hearing so many damn gunshots. Now I hear 'em so much I done got used to it. I hardly flinched when that gun went off a few hours ago, and now look. Right down the street. Another body. Another man done lost his life over some nonsense. It's ridiculous."

"Tell me about it. I saw it go down. The nigga who did it ditched the damn gun in my auntie's bedroom closet. I told her she better keep them young boys out of her house before she ends up getting jammed up behind some of their shit. Excuse my language."

"Girl, you a grown woman. Talk how you talk. I'm forty-one, not seventy-one." Maria grabbed a twenty-ounce bottle of Sprite out of the fridge and walked out of the kitchen with her plate in hand and a curious expression on her face.

She wanted to know more about the gun in Shanita's bedroom closet, mostly to see whether or not her sons were involved, but also to be nosy.

"Yeah, but anyway, I've been in Kansas. Had a bum-ass boyfriend who stole all my stuff. I'm about to start dancing at that club on 16th and Trumbull if shit don't go right with this lil tax scheme I got going."

"Wait, back it up a little." Maria sat down and cracked open her Sprite. "Who shot the boy up the street? At least I hope it was a boy. I hope to God it ain't Erica."

Ciara sucked her teeth and put on a mask of disgust. "I wish it was that bitch. She's the main reason I left in the first place. Couldn't believe it when they told me Rell was fucking her behind my back. That lil nasty hoe was already fucking and sucking on everything moving way back then. Heard she's a cokehead now."

"So who was it? Who got killed?"

"I don't know. Some boy who worked for a nigga Rell n'em into it with. Guess they whacked him to get back at the nigga. I really don't know a lot about it. I ain't been back in the city too long, and all them boys left my auntie's house after that went down. Now her dumb self is sitting down there all paranoid and shit, worried she gon' get caught with that big-ass gun in her closet. I hope this teaches her a lesson. Her ass is way too old to be having all them young-ass boys in her house like that. I'm about to find me somewhere else to stay until I get back on my feet, 'cause I ain't gon' be able to deal with that mess every day. I could barely even sleep last night with all the noise they was making."

"You're welcome to stay here if you want," Maria said, and she meant it. With Rell and Jah no longer living with her, her days had suddenly gotten lonely, and she figured it would be good to have some company. Especially a fine young girl like Ciara, a girl from the neighborhood who knew all the dirt that was going on in the streets. Maria was always trying to find out what was going on with the youngsters. Rell and Jah never told her anything.

"No, I couldn't do that," Ciara said, shaking her head. "Rell's engaged. I heard he just proposed to the girl yesterday. I'd be crossing the line moving in with you."

"Girl, boo." Maria waved off Ciara's words and took a bite of her sausage. She chewed and swallowed. "This is my house. I pay all the bills in here. And now that I'm not an assistant anymore, my pay will be over a quarter million a year. I just reached an agreement with the owner of this house to buy it in cash for a hundred and forty. This is where I'll be staying for the long run, honey. The people upstairs can stay, but now they gotta pay me. I'ma try to buy a few more houses on this block to make it a safer place to stay. First time I see some damn gangbangers hanging outside of 'em, I'm putting their asses out. You can go and get your bags and move right into Jah's bedroom. It's already empty and ready for you. I ain't taking no for an answer."

For a moment, Ciara just stared at Maria, wearing a smirk with one brow lifted. Then she laughed and shook her head.

"So," Ciara asked, "what made Rell wanna marry that girl? I couldn't believe it when I heard he had proposed to Tamera Lyon. I remember back when Tamera used to live in that building on Douglas."

"That's Rell and Jah's building now. Big Man left it to them."

"How in the world did Big Man get a building? He was strung out on that dog food when I left."

"He got his act together and married that crazy old lady. They started buying up buildings and houses, all kinds of investments. Made a nice chunk of change. Left it all to Rell and Jah. Hell, they're set for life now. I'm glad. Keep their asses out of my pockets. Bad enough I gotta deal with Jah's little evil twin. And speaking of that little devil"— Maria got up and headed toward her bedroom — "let me see what the hell she's in here doing. She's too quiet."

When Maria made it to her bedroom she stopped in the doorway, put her hands on her hips, and gawked at Dora.

The jar of Vaseline that had been sitting on Maria's nightstand was on the floor at Dora's feet. It was empty, and all the Vaseline was on Dora's face and hands.

"Lil girl, what the hell is wrong with you?"

Dora gasped and fell to the floor at the sound of Maria's voice. She looked up at her grandmother with guilty eyes and immediately started crying.

"I'm about to give you something to cry about," Maria said.

She was just reaching for Dora's hand to pick her up and give her a fair amount of swats to the bottom when she heard a laugh behind her.

It was Ciara.

"I can see now that it's going to be fun staying here," Ciara said, crossing her arms over her chest and laughing hysterically.

King Rio

Chapter 8

"Apple's on his way home from the hospital," Jah said as he read the text message he'd just received on his smartphone.

He immediately set the phone aside and picked the remote to the PlayStation 4 back up. He was playing Grand Theft Auto 5.

Rell was sitting beside him with his own iPhone in hand, checking out the prices on used cars. He wanted a Mercedes Benz S550, like the rental he had parked outside. He had the money to buy a brand-new one but wasn't willing to waste $130,000 when he could get a nice two-year-old used one for $50,000 or less.

"Cut this dumb-ass game off. We need to be going to check on Apple."

"Nigga, he lives right across the street."

"So what? We gotta go, anyway. I need to drop this work off to Johnny B and Lil Larry. Then I'm taking that rental back to the dealership and buying one. I want you to grab one, too. That way we'll be pulling up back to back in Benzes. Two all-black S550s. Come summertime, we can throw some sixes on em and ball."

Jah paused the game and looked over at Rell, nodding his head thoughtfully. "Hell yeah. On Neal. Shit, ain't nobody in the hood riding like that. We'll fuck up the game. Have these niggas looking at us like Cup and Cholly used to be."

"RIP to them," Rell said. He and Charles "Lil Cholly" Duff had been close friends, and he'd also had a good rapport with Cup, whose son now owned the strip club up the street. Cup and Lil Cholly had been plugged with a Mexican drug cartel that kept them so flooded with bricks of cocaine and heroin that they ran the city's drug trade all the way up to the day they were both shot and killed inside The Visionary Lounge, another nightclub that now belonged to Cup's son.

"You know," Jah said as they stood to leave, "they say Cup got rich off the ransom money he got from kidnapping that nigga Bulletface's daughter. Before Bulletface was even a rapper."

Rell shrugged and took a look out the living room windows.

Bulletface was the wealthiest rapper in the game now, worth more than a billion dollars, and his wife, an entertainment tycoon named Alexus Costilla, was wealthier than Bill Gates. It was rumored that Alexus was the boss of a Mexican drug cartel. Rell had once watched a CNN special about it.

Cup's son, known all throughout the city as Bankroll Reese, had inherited Cup's fortune. Bankroll Reese was the only young nigga on the west side of Chicago who had all kinds of foreign cars and expensive diamond jewelry. He was rumored to have inherited almost $80 million.

Although Rell was pretty sure that he would never be as rich as Bankroll Reese, he knew that it would feel great to look like he was as rich. He and Jah were the next best thing. There wasn't anybody else riding through the hood in Mercedes Benzes.

"I wanna slide over there and see if we can catch Tremaine, too," Jah said as they walked out the door. "That nigga ain't getting away with raping my girl. Soon's I see his ass, it's game over."

Rell had put some salt on the porch to clear up the snow. He felt it crunching beneath his sneakers as they walked down the stairs.

The Glock was heavy on his hip, so heavy that it made his sweatpants sag and he had to keep pulling them up. He saw the car full of Jah's friends parked across the street. They gave a nod and went back to talking to each other.

"Lil bro n'em poled up," Jah said as they got in the Benz. "Baby and Tamera gon' be straight. A nigga'll be a damn fool to ride up on this block on some bullshit. My lil hittas got two Ks and they can't wait to let 'em blow."

"Just make sure that they don't leave. 24/7 means just that. No sleeping, no none of that."

"Bruh, will you let me take care of this? Damn, nigga. I got this. Let's ride, nigga."

Reluctantly, Rell started the engine and drove away from his home. He cruised to the corner of 15th and Trumbull and then kept going forward to Douglas Boulevard. He was a little worried about Tamera's safety, but since he knew that she and Tirzah were about to go to his cousin Tara's house in a few minutes, he let it go. Jah was right. They would be fine.

As he was steering the Mercedes down Douglas Boulevard, Jah got a call from Momma. He put it on speakerphone, and both of them laughed as soon as she spoke.

"Jah, you son of a bitch, if you don't get your ass over here and pick up this bad-ass lil girl, I'ma kill her."

Jah fell against his door, laughing uncontrollably and slapping a hand on his knee.

"What she do now, Ma?" Rell asked.

"This lil crazy-ass baby done dumped chips all on my floor, covered herself in Vaseline, ran from me when I tried to spank her. And she knows exactly what she's doing because she gets that guilty-ass look on her face every time you catch her doing wrong. Jah, you need a second DNA test. That first one had to be wrong. I cannot be related to this lil devil here. Jah, get'cha ass over here. I'm serious, now. Quit that damn laughing. I don't see a damn thing funny."

"It's hilarious to me," Jah said, finally catching his breath. "And if I'm a son of a bitch, then—"

Rell punched Jah in the arm before he could complete the sentence.

"Do me a favor, Rell, and beat his ass for me, will you? I'll pay cash money."

"We on our way over there, Ma. Gimme five minutes."

"One minute late and this lil girl will be making snow angels," Maria threatened before ending the call.

Jah seemed unable to stop laughing.

After connecting his iPhone to the Bluetooth, Rell turned on Rick Ross's *Black Market* album and bumped "Foreclosures" while he drove to Momma's house, keeping his eyes peeled for any signs of Zo and the other members of the Spaulding clique.

It felt odd beefing with guys who were in the same gang that he was in, but he knew that that was how the game went these days. In the streets of Chicago, just about everyone had mob ties, and one little disagreement or altercation could set off a never-ending war. He and Jah were into it with the Spaulding set of TVLs and they were also at odds with the Conservative Vice Lords on 16th and Millard. They were living just blocks away from both of the gangs that they had beef with. Now that Rell thought about it, maybe Tamera's idea to move away from the hood was his best move.

He ruminated over his next move while listening to the music and cruising up the boulevard.

"Had it all, now it's repossessed
Can't feed the clique cutting bad checks
Time to learn, boy, that cash rules
Success is a precious jewel..."

Rell's musical mood was suddenly ruined when he saw all the police on 13th and Avers. He quickly took the long clip out of his pistol and slipped both the clip and the Glock in his hoodie's pocket. Then he zipped his black leather Pelle Pelle jacket closed.

Jah's Mac-10 had a shoulder strap that he draped around his neck before zipping up his own jacket, which was also a black leather Pelle, though the design was slightly different from Rell's. He grinned and said, "Damn, big bruh. Look like a nigga done got whacked or some shit."

Shaking his head at Jah's foolishness, Rell pushed open his door and stepped out of the car.

Every cop on the block looked at him and Jah as they crossed the street to Momma's house.

The nervousness was real.

Rell kept his eyes on his smartphone, as did Jah. It was the most regular thing to do. Nowadays, everyone walked around with their eyes on their phones. Rell hoped that the Benz would persuade the policemen to leave him and Jah alone. No gangbangers were driving around the Lawndale neighborhood in Benzes. They would think that Rell and Jah were business owners of some sort. At least, that's what Rell hoped they would think.

He knew one thing for sure. He was not leaving Momma's house until the police were gone.

King Rio

Chapter 9

"That nigga raped me, sis. I wanna fucking...aghhhhh! He fucked with the wrong bitch! I'm telling you, I won't rest until that nigga is resting in peace. I'll do his ass just like you did Tangie and Shalonda. Straight dome shot his old lame ass and take his money."

Tamera could hear her sister crying through the bathroom door, and she was pissed that it was locked.

"Girl, will you open up this door so I can talk to you? Calm down, alright? That nigga is definitely going to get what he has coming. You breaking down on me isn't going to help at all, though, so get it together. Unlock the door, Tirz."

She heard Tirzah's sniffles. Then the doorknob moved and the door opened. She stepped in just as Tirzah put her back against the wall and slid down to the floor with her face buried in the palms of her hands.

Tamera sat down next to her and put an arm around her shoulder. She hugged Tirzah close and whispered, "I'm here, sis. Me and you can fight the whole world and win as long as we stay strong. We can't break down. If we break down, we lose. If we break down, bitch niggas like Tremaine win. You're not trying to lose, are you? Because I'm not. I'm trying to win at everything we do."

Another sniffle from Tirzah. "I'm good," she murmured. "It's just that...he raped me yesterday. You don't know how weak I felt when that shit happened to me. You know I've always been a fighter. I've never even lost a fight. When that nigga threw me down, I tried to fight back against his old ass, but he was so strong. I can't believe he was so strong. I guess I underestimated him."

"He's a man, Tirzah. No matter his age. Don't feel bad. We'll get him. Mark my words, he is going to get what he deserves when it's all said and done. Clean up your face so we can get out of here. After we stop by Tara's house, we can go over to K Town and look for the nigga ourselves."

Tirzah stood up and went to the sink. They were in the bathroom of Jah's upstairs apartment. It was similar to the one Tamera shared with Rell downstairs, just slightly less tidy and more cluttered. Tirzah had never been much into house cleaning, and apparently Jah shared the same trait. Just last week, Tamera had cleaned their whole apartment because she'd grown tired of coming up here and seeing their rooms so messy.

She grabbed a handful of Tirzah's ass and gave it a squeeze.

Tirzah snickered. "Bitch, if you don't get your hand off my booty."

"It's getting fatter. You're thicker than I am now. Jah been hitting these groceries? Huh? He been sticking his penis in your bottom?"

"You're retarded, Tam. You really are."

"I'm not retarded. I'm just good at noticing shit like this."

"Why are we going to Tara's? I thought she was coming over here with K?"

"We're meeting her over there just to kick it for a little while. To keep you from crying in your bathroom like a little bitch. Toughen up. Once you get that liquor in your system, I bet your ass won't be crying. You'll be running over there to Tremaine's house to bust his head wide the fuck open."

Tirzah shook her head. "Call and tell her to just meet us here like we planned. We gotta go up the street for my interview at Redbone's. They emailed me back this morning and said they like my pictures. I'm supposed to go in for the interview at four o'clock."

Crossing her arms and squinting at Tirzah's reflection in the sink mirror, Tamera said, "Are you fucking serious?"

"Don't act surprised, Tam. We talked about this a hundred times before. I can't keep depending on Jah's young ass to take care of me. And that fifty grand is almost gone. Neither of us have jobs. If Rell and Jah cut us off for some reason, we'd be out in the streets by the end of summer unless one of us is able to find a job. I don't wanna go through that. I've danced before. I know that Jah and Rell got money, but I'm independent like I've always been. I wanna make my own money."

"Nothing wrong with being independent, but that's just dumb. Your man is a millionaire now."

"You're right. He's a millionaire, and I'm trying to be a millionaire just like him. I just gotta meet Bankroll Reese while he's in town. Shouldn't take no more than a couple of minutes."

There was no way that Tamera was going to agree with Tirzah on this one, but right or wrong, she was sticking to her big sister's side. If Tirzah wanted to go back to stripping, then Tamera was going to be Tirzah's biggest fan.

"Have you told Jah about you going back to stripping?"

Tirzah shook her head no. "Gotta make sure I get the job first. Ain't no sense in arguing with that crazy-ass nigga over something I ain't even got yet."

"Jah is going to strangle you."

"No, he ain't gonna do shit to me. What he's going to do is respect my hustle. As long as he knows that I ain't fucking none of those lame-ass niggas that be up in that club, he shouldn't have a problem with me making my own money. It'll keep me from spending his."

"Girl, that nigga just put a ring on your finger in front of thousands of people at the United Center last night. Now you're going to an interview for a job as a stripper?" Tamera shook her head incredulously. "It just doesn't add up. It sounds so foolish to me. You're making a mistake."

Tirzah turned to look at Tamera. "He might've made it right and proposed to me last night, but let's not forget that he broke up with me yesterday morning. On fucking Valentine's Day. If he'd have stuck with his decision, I would be homeless or living with you and Rell right now. He's the one who made me decide to give dancing another try. Don't try and make me out to be the bad one, because his ass is just as guilty as I am."

Tamera was not going to get anywhere with Tirzah, so she turned and headed out of the bathroom. "Just bring your ass on so we can go. Dumb ass."

"Your momma's dumb," Tirzah retorted.

Tamera didn't point out the fact that they shared the same mother. Instead, she went to the living room window and glanced out to the street below. She looked both ways. There was snow everywhere, but the sun was out and the snow was melting. Her shiny gray Corvette looked amazing parked down there at the curb. She eyed a car that was parked across the street with its motor running and figured it was the guys Jah had paid to watch the house. One of them was sitting on the hood of the car, smoking a cigarette and thumbing through his smartphone. Tamera wondered if his bare hands were cold.

What if his hands were too cold to pull his gun if somebody drove by shooting?

She opened the window and shouted, "Hey! Get back in that car! What if somebody drives past trying to shoot my damn door up again and your damn fingers are half frozen?"

The boy looked up at her and scoffed at the shrewd order. "What if you sit down somewhere and let us take care of this shit. We got two mu'fuckin' AKs for a nigga. Let us do what bro paid us to do. You just sit in there and be pretty."

Tamera was grinding her teeth together in anger as she slammed the window shut and stomped off to the dining room table where her MK bag was sitting. She took her Glock handgun out of the bag and aimed it at the living room window as she sat down. Then she put down the gun and picked up her smartphone. She called Tara.

"Yoooooo," Tara answered.

"Girl, I am so done with everything in my life right now," Tamera said.

"Ooooh shit, bitch, spill the tea."

"Well," Tamera began, "first of all, I won't be meeting you at your house because this thot I call my sister is going down to the strip club on 16th for a damn job interview."

"What?"

"I know, right?"

"Tirzah's about to start stripping?"

"Mm-hmm. With her dumb ass."

"Jah will come to that club and kill every nigga in that bitch."

"Trust me, she knows that shit. She knows exactly how Jah gets down and yet she wants to play games like he won't pull it. She ain't even told him about it yet."

"Oh, Lord. Let me know how that works out. I guarantee it's gon' get ugly."

"I tried to tell her ass that."

"You want me to just come over there now? Maybe me and you together can talk some sense into her crazy ass."

"Nah, that interview is in like fifteen minutes. And you know Redbone's ain't nowhere from our house."

From the bathroom Tirzah shouted, "I hear that shit!"

Tara said, "I don't give a fuck what she heard. Tamera, put me on speakerphone so I can talk to her nutty ass myself, 'cause I see now that she got me so fucked up. I don't do no behind-the-back talking. This ain't the NBA. I ain't throwing no special passes. This is all a hundred percent Tara, baby. I don't know what the fuck she thought, but I'll set her straight right damn now."

Tamera busted out laughing. "It ain't that serious. I got this shit handled. I'ma go up there to the strip club with her dumb ass and I'ma sabotage the whole play."

"That's what I'm talking about, bitch. Don't let her do no dumb shit like that. My lil cousin just got down on one knee and proposed to her yesterday. I'm pretty sure he wasn't planning on marrying a stripper."

"I got this shit covered, Cuz. Don't even worry about it."

"Oh, and I wanted to tell you something," Tara added. "Did Rell ever tell you about Cee Cee? His old girlfriend?"

"Cee Cee?" Tamera frowned. "No. He told me about Erica, but I ain't heard about no Cee Cee."

"Okay, well, he was in love with this lil girl named Ciara back when he was like fifteen, sixteen. We called her Lil Booty Cee Cee 'cause the bitch didn't have no ass. Anyway, the bitch just got back in town, and I know she's gonna be all on Rell if and when she sees him, so watch out for that hoe. She's just as pretty as you, and I hear she even got a lil ass on her now. You know how dumb niggas go for a fat ass. Watch out for that bitch. Just giving you a warning."

"Girl, please. I ain't worried about no bitch. Trust me when I say that I got Rell wrapped around my finger. Literally. That nigga won't dare cheat on me."

"Okay, bitch. Don't say I didn't tell you."

Tamera stared at her iPhone 6S for a long time after the call with Tara ended, wondering who this Cee Cee chick was and whether or not she was someone to be worried about.

Chapter 10

When Rell walked in the door and saw Ciara sitting on the sofa, his mouth fell agape and his eyes went wide with surprise.

"The fuck are you doing here in my momma's house? And where the hell is she at?"

Ciara laughed and pointed to the hallway that led to the bathroom and bedrooms. "She's back there giving Dora a bath. Dora got into the Vaseline. Funniest shit I've seen in a long time."

Rell stared at Ciara, while Jah headed off to the bathroom.

Ciara looked beautiful.

She was sitting with her legs crossed, a half-eaten Polish sausage on the coffee table in front of her. There were rips in the knees of her jeans. Her makeup was impeccably done. Her hair was short and choppy and dyed light brown. Her shirt was a long-sleeved black fabric with a red photo of Derrick Rose on its chest. She was on her Samsung Galaxy smartphone, inboxing someone on Facebook. She hardly even gave him a glance.

"The fuck are you doing over here?" Rell asked her as he shut and locked the door behind him.

Ciara shrugged her shoulders. "Came over here to see your mom. Got bored down there at my auntie Shanita's house. Plus, I gotta admit, I was a little scared. More than a little. With all these cops on the block and the murder weapon in the house with us I had to leave. I couldn't just stay there."

Rell nodded. "I feel you." He sat down and picked up the Polish sausage and took a huge bite.

"Nigga." Ciara looked at him. "How you just gon' bite my damn sausage without asking?"

"Oh." He chewed. "Didn't know." More chewing. "Didn't know it was yours. Thought it was Momma's."

"Just kidding. It actually is hers. Still disrespectful to just take a bite out of her sausage, though."

"That's my momma. I'll take a bite out of any damn thing I want to in this mu'fucka."

Rell drank a swallow of the cold Sprite that stood next to Momma's plate just as Maria came strolling in from the hallway, drying her hands on a bath towel.

"Rell," Maria said, "that lil bad-ass niece of yours gotta go. No more babysitting for me. You better tell Jah to start paying one of these lil girls around here, 'cause I ain't going for it no more. I'ma be done lost my damn mind messing around with her. She's the devil, you hear me? The devil."

Apparently, Maria was in no mood to ask Rell to get out of her seat. She simply grabbed ahold of the collar of his jacket and pulled until he rose from the sofa. He laughed and got out of the way.

"Ma, what's wrong with you?" he said. "Dora couldn't have made you this crazy."

"I'm on vacation from my job, Rell. This is the first day of my two-week vacation. I'm supposed to be relaxing. I just saw my granddaughter's momma laid out on a table with her whole chest cut open. I shouldn't have to come home to no shit like this."

While Maria put her lighter to the end of a cigarette and lit up, Ciara smiled at her phone. Rell had a feeling that Ciara was smiling at the way Maria had just talked to him. He could smell Ciara's perfume. It smelled delicious. Her jacket was draped over the arm of the sofa. Her purse was open on the coffee table.

Rell circled the table to take a peek in her purse. He found himself wondering what she had been up to these last seven years or so. How many men she'd fucked. How many ballers she'd set up. How many other scandalous things she'd done. He wondered if living in a different state, far away from her friends and family here in Chicago, had changed her in any way. He had taken Ciara's virginity when they were thirteen, and he hoped that it was still a special memory to her.

She looked up at him and frowned. "What are you eye-balling my purse for?" she asked with a voice full of attitude.

Rell showed her a grin.

"It ain't funny, boy. Maria, please get your lil nosy son."

"Leave this girl alone, Rell. Go and call your wife."

"Yeah, what she said." Ciara chuckled.

Rell wanted to put both of them in check, but instead he nodded and headed for the bathroom with Jah.

He was right on time.

His phone rang just as he made it to the bathroom door. Tamera was calling.

He answered, "What's up, baby?"

"Where you at?" She sounded like she was getting ready to snap on him.

"At my OG crib."

"Who the fuck is Ciara?"

His eyes got wide. How'd Tamera know about Ciara?

"Why you ask that?"

"Because I heard she's your ex and that she's back in town. Because I'ma kill you and that bitch if I find out you done been anywhere near her. That's why. Got any more questions?"

"Baby, don't start trippin' already. Chill out with that shit. I didn't even know she was here in the city." Rell leaned back on the wall, looked into the bathroom, and saw Jah taking Dora out of the bathtub.

"Just do the right thing like Spike Lee," Tamera said, "because if you go around that bitch at all, it's gon' be something serious. I'm trying my best to remember who that hoe is. I know I remember that name from somewhere."

"Baby...you ain't got shit to worry about. Me and lil bruh about to slide down on that nigga in K-Town and try to catch him out there so we can get that shit over with. Y'all just stay in the house, or go to Tara's house — whatever. Just make sure y'all ain't out in these streets 'cause it's ugly out here and niggas ain't ducking shit."

"I love you, Rell."

"I love you, too. Stop trippin'. Lil crazy-ass girl. I'll be back home in no time. Would've just brought you with me if I knew you was gon' start going nuts over some dumb shit."

"Oh, whatever. I told you beforehand that I had a few screws loose. Sorry, bae." She kissed him through the phone before he pressed end.

He dropped his head back and closed his eyes to think. He and Jah had long money now and they were engaged to two of the most beautiful women in Chicago, but they were still trapped in the streets. They were still riding around the city with guns on them, ready to shoot whenever they ran across their enemies. As bad as he wanted to just marry Tamera and live happily ever after, Rell knew that Zo had to be taken out. Zo was too much of a threat. He had too much money, and he was angry with Jah about Roddy's murder. Not to mention the fact that Zo knew where Rell and Jah lived.

Maybe Tamera was right. Maybe they needed to move out of the house on Trumbull Avenue at their earliest convenience. Maybe they needed to go to another neighborhood or another city until the hits they had on Zo and Tremaine were tended to. He had a feeling that something was going to happen very soon in retaliation for the murder of Zo's worker, and definitely for the murder of Zo's brother.

"We just gotta go, lil bruh," Rell said. "We gotta pack up and get the fuck away from this drama. We got weddings that we need to be getting ready for, families to start and provide for. It ain't gon' work with us living here in the hood. I know it ain't gon' work. The only thing out here for niggas like us is jail and death, and I don't want neither one of em."

It took Jah half a minute to reply, which was good. He was seriously thinking things over in that hard head of his as he put a fresh pair of clothes on his daughter.

"I was thinking the same shit, big bruh. No lie. We gotta sit down and figure out what we gon' do with this money before we end up blowing it. I think we should just get a few more houses and keep collecting rent for a while. That's like having a guaranteed job without having to work. I'm already loving those fat-ass checks every month. See if we can get another apartment building or two."

"Now, that's the kind of talk I like to hear." Rell's spirit was lifted by Jah's ideas. He looked over at Jah. "And we gotta get out of the habit of dressing like street niggas. We gotta go and grab us some suits and ties. Get into the corporate world of—"

"Hey, hey, hey." Jah held up a hand to stop Rell. "I was with you until you hit me with that dress code. I'm a street nigga, bruh. I can dress fresh and still do business. Balmains, Trues, and Robin's, nigga. And Pelle."

Rell laughed. "Okay. That's cool. Well, I'll be the corporate-looking brother and you can just do you. But the first thing we gotta do is get out of Lawndale. I'm thinking the South Loop. That'll keep us in the city but far enough away from the hood to avoid all the nonsense."

Jah made eye contact with Rell as he was putting on Dora's shirt. "You just wanna get away from Ciara's ass before you fuck around and mess up what you got going with Tamera. That's why your ass is hiding in the hallway like that."

"How the fuck am I hiding?" Rell said, though he realized that he might be doing just that.

"Her lil ass done got thick," Jah said. "And she always been pretty in the face. Lil sexy ass. Don't even lie and say you don't wanna fuck."

"I don't. All I wanna do is go home to Tamera every night. That's it."

Jah walked to the doorway with Dora on his hip and stared at Rell with disbelieving eyes.

"What?" Rell said.

"Nigga, you know what. You got a bad bitch sitting in your momma's living room, and you still got a bedroom in this mu'fucka. That's what."

Dora reached a hand out to Rell and, in her standard gibberish, said, "Muh. Fuh. Muh fuh."

"Bad word!" Rell said, swatting his fingertips at Dora's mouth.

He and Jah laughed.

Dora laughed with them.

They went to the living room with Momma and Ciara.

Rell took a chair from the dining table and brought it to the living room to keep himself as far away from Ciara as humanly possible.

74

Chapter 11

There were just two young couples and a middle-aged Black guy in a faded John Deere cap sitting at the restaurant's tables when Zo walked into the McDonald's on Kedzie and Roosevelt Road. He ordered a Big Mac and a large Coke and then sat down and waited.

It was ten minutes later when the tall young man with dreadlocks came in and strolled through the restaurant to Zo's table. By then, Zo was already done eating the Big Mac and halfway finished with the soda.

The young man's name was Johnny B. He sat across from Zo and drummed his fingernails on the table.

"What up, joe?" Johnny B said. "Where my Big Mac?"

"You'll be able to buy a lifetime supply of Big Macs when you make this shit happen," Zo said. He slurped his soda through a straw. "About how long do I gotta wait? 'Cause I can do the shit myself if it's gon' take you too long."

"First off, nigga, don't be talking down to me like I'm some kinda pussy boy. I'm a shooter, lil nigga. You ain't even eighteen yet. Respect yo' elders."

"Jah ain't eighteen, either. I was in the same class with that nigga. And age ain't got shit to do with nothing. All I wanna know is when it's gon' get done, 'cause like I said, I can really do it myself. Shit, I can really just pay one of my lil homies to do it."

"Really? How? Tell me how the fuck you gon' accomplish that when they got pistols, choppas, and 24/7 security. If anything, it's gon' be a gunfight. You ain't gon' be able to just catch 'em slippin'. Trust me, it's gon' have to be somebody who's close to 'em to do it if it's gon' get done at all. Who better than me? Just run me that bread and gimme a lil time to get the shit thought out. You can leave town for a few weeks to clear your name out of it. I'ma get the job done. No questions about it."

Zo drank more soda, studying Johnny B's expression. He didn't trust Johnny B and he was sure Johnny B didn't trust him either. But he knew that Johnny B needed the money. Johnny B didn't even have a car. Rell and Jah weren't feeding their guys the way Zo was feeding his. Zo's team was eating good. All of them were dressed fresh every day, and most of them had cars. They had all the girls. All the other cliques hated on them because of the way they were winning in the dope game.

The same could not be said for Rell and Jah's D-Block squad. Zo had heard this morning that Rell and Jah were riding around flexing in an S550 Benz, but none of their guys were riding like them. Hell, their guys weren't riding at all.

Zo had a feeling that the reason the Owens brothers weren't feeding their block was because Rell had gotten out of the game after doing some time in prison, and since Rell was trying to be a family man, Jah was following in his brother's footsteps.

That was their weakness.

That was why Johnny B was now sitting at the table with Zo, trying to work out a deal to whack one of his own guys.

"So," Zo asked, easing back in his chair, "how long is this shit gon' take? How soon should I expect to wait for this shit to get done?"

"It ain't gon' take me long." Johnny B's eyes moved about nervously. Obviously he was worried that someone would see him meeting with Zo and report back to Jah with the information. "Look, just gimme the bread so we can get this show on the road. I need $50,000 instead of the $30,000 you offered. I'll pick the perfect time and off the nigga. No worries."

"Nah, it don't work like that." Zo took a rubber-banded knot of cash out of his pocket and handed it to Johnny B. "That's $10,000. I'll give you the rest when it's done. You got two weeks."

"The rest?"

"Yeah, the rest. The other $20,000. That was the deal."

"Nah. I need fifty racks, bruh. Fifty racks or I ain't on shit. I know how much bread you been making over there on Spaulding. Ain't nobody stupid. Pay me what it's worth. I might catch a life bid for this shit. I ain't going for no less than fifty racks. Period."

Zo finished off the soda and swiped the cup aside. He and Johnny B stared into each other's eyes for a couple of seconds.

Lisa, Zo's girlfriend's best friend, walked past and said, "Hey, Zo. Hey, Johnny B."

Neither of them spoke back to her.

"Look, nigga," Johnny B snapped. "You got me in here bogus as fuck, got bitches seeing me talking to you and shit. Let me know now what it's gon' be. I ain't with all this bull-shit."

"Who killed my lil homie on D Block?"

"What? Man, what the fuck you talking about? What's that got to do with Jah?"

"I just wanna know. Who killed James on Erica's porch?"

"You really wanna know?" Johnny B looked around the restaurant. "A'ight. Capone. My lil nigga Capone whacked him."

"Okay." Zo nodded his head and stood up to leave. "Whack Capone and Jah and I'll give you the fifty. I'm gone. Two weeks."

Zo didn't say another word. He left out of McDonald's and got in his Cadillac and drove out of the parking lot without looking back, feeling confident that he had just set the wheels in motion to finally get the revenge his little brother Roddy deserved.

Chapter 12

After spending the past week and a half partying with a wealthy friend of his in Dubai, eighteen-year-old Tyrese "Bankroll Reese" Harrison was feeling drowsy and out of it.

He was leaning back in the leather swivel chair with his feet kicked up on his glass-top desk, snoozing and dreaming about the three beautiful Iranian models he'd made love to on his private jet while in Dubai. He'd had a different trio of women in his suite at the Dubai Marriott Harbour Hotel, but none of them could compare to the Iranian models who'd given him a good time on the jet. He had their phone numbers. He would definitely be calling them during his next trip to the rich oil country.

Reese had gone through a lot since his father's murder, but he was a strong young man who was hard to break. He had endured all the pain of losing his dad with a straight face and a cool demeanor. Many would argue that the only reason he took the grief so easily was because he was now richer than most people could ever dream of being, but that wasn't the case at all. The truth of the matter was, he had come up in the Lawndale neighborhood with all the rest of the poor people. He was humble because he had gone without as a kid. It was not until his father was released from prison when he was twelve years old that Reese began to get a taste of the good life, a direct result of the connections his father had formed with Mexico's reigning drug cartel.

The millions of dollars in drug money had been laundered through a number of different businesses, and now it all belonged to Reese. His net worth was $57 million. He'd already been in *Forbes* magazine twice since his father's passing. He had yet to purchase a single car or home because he had all the cars and homes his father had owned. He was brown-skinned and handsome and slightly arrogant, but humble and grateful nonetheless, and he loved interacting with people, which is why he had no problem working at the numerous nightclubs he now owned.

Today he wore a finely tailored gold-and-black Versace shirt over black slacks and croc skin Mauri shoes. His jewelry consisted of an obnoxiously thick gold chain that was just as drenched in crushed white diamonds as its pendant, which was a gold depiction of his father's face; a 20-carat yellow diamond pinky ring; and an icy Audemers watch. His hair was cut in a low lying fade. His facial hair was neatly trimmed. He was not one of those millionaires who looked good because of his money. He'd already had the good looks before the wealth.

Chubb and Suwu, Reese's armed bodyguards, were also snoozing. They were in a pair of chairs on the other side of the office, clad in black suits, their heads dropping and lifting and dropping again as they struggled against sleep.

Reese's eyes cracked open at the sound of a knock on his office door. A glance at his watch was all it took to let him know who it was. He had three girls looking to start working here at Redbone's, one of the four strip clubs he owned.

One of the girls was Tirzah Lyon.

Reese had put her first on the interview list.

He and all of his childhood friends had been fantasizing about fucking her ever since they were preteens. Tirzah was the baddest girl in the North Lawndale neighborhood. Her sister was also a bad bitch, but Tirzah was the epitome of dime piece in Reese's eyes.

"Come in," he said, moving his feet to the floor and blinking away the sleep.

Elana, his personal assistant, pushed open the door and stepped in ahead of Tirzah and Tamera.

"I'm sorry," Elana said, "but she insisted on bringing her sister in with her."

"It's fine. You can leave us." Reese leaned forward, feeling almost hypnotized by Tirzah's unprecedented beauty. She wore the same kind of tight jeans that her sister had on.

"Hey, Reese," Tirzah said cheerfully as she and Tamera walked to his desk.

"Stop right there. Don't sit down yet. Turn around. Let me see it," Reese said.

His mouth watered as Tirzah stopped in front of the chair across the desk from him and did a slow spin. Her body was so perfectly curvaceous, and her face was so flawless. He had no doubt that she would be the baddest dancer in Redbone's. None of the other girls were as bad as Tirzah. None of them had the cakes she possessed. None of them were as pretty. He could tell by the look on her face that she knew she was the baddest chick in the game.

"I know, I know," she said as she turned to face him. "I'm a bad bitch. Perfect for your club. And I've done this shit before, so I know how it goes. I know I'ma have some bitches hating on me in this bitch, and I know you're gonna have a bunch of guys requesting to see me every night. I'm okay with all of that. The only thing I ask is for you to make sure that I get a sixty-forty split on the money — sixty my way, forty yours — and a full-time bodyguard while I'm in here. And not one of those lazy fucks over there."

Tirzah cast a glance at the sleeping giants across the room from them.

Nodding his head, Reese looked from Tirzah to Tamera and back to Tirzah again.

"Any chance I could get both of you to—"

"No way in hell," Tamera said quickly.

"Oh, no. She's not a dancer," Tirzah explained. "She's my sister."

"I know who she is," Reese said. "I've known y'all since I was a little boy. Remember when my OG stayed downstairs from y'all in the building on Douglas? Me and my cousins used to come up there and knock on your door just to see you and her. I'll never forget who y'all are."

Reese had four separate stacks of bank-new packets of hundred-dollar bills on the desk before him. He also had two white iPhones, one plugged up to a charger, the other lighting up incessantly as call after call came in.

He picked up two packets of hundreds and launched them at his bodyguards. One missed and hit the wall over Chubb's shoulder, and the other one struck Suwu right on the forehead. Both of the big guys jumped to their feet, nearly colliding with each other as they stood up to see what was going on.

"If you two fat muthafuckas don't wake up. I could be getting robbed right now. Sleep at home, not on the job in my office."

Chubb, a brown-skinned Goliath of a man with a low-top fade and an endless supply of jokes, said, "Lil nigga, I'm old enough to be yo' daddy. Throw something else at me and see if I don't treat you like I treat my sons."

"For real," Suwu added. He was darker and just as heavyset, and at 6'1" he stood a few inches shorter than Chubb. "Damn near gave me a heart attack."

"I'ma give y'all asses something. Ain't gon' be a heart attack," Reese said, shifting his attention back to Tirzah as she and Tamera sat down across the desk from him.

He was already fantasizing about the things he'd like to do to Tirzah. He knew that he would enjoy a night with her, and if it were at all possible, he was going to try and make it happen. He could already see himself kissing his way down from her neck to her breasts to the meal between her thighs.

"How old are you again?" he asked her.

"Older than you."

"That's not what I asked."

"I know what you asked," Tirzah said.

"Well, can I have an answer? I need that kind of information from all my girls."

"I'm not just any girl, Reese. You know who I am. You just said so yourself. I'm just here to get some money. I don't necessarily need this job, but I want it. If you're going to give me shit about being hired, I'll gladly go somewhere else."

Reese smiled. He had a perfect smile, thanks to the dental work he'd had done just a few weeks ago.

"You know that I won't be here most of the time, right?" he said. "You might be able to get away with talking to me like this, but I'm telling you now, my bro Luke ain't going for it. He'll cuss your ass clean out about that attitude and send you straight home. Just warning you. Be mindful of how and when you use that attitude."

Tirzah rolled her eyes and crossed her arms over her chest. The right side of her mouth drew back in a smirk. She stared at Reese and waited for him to continue.

She looked so sexy waiting like that.

"May I ask one more question?" he said. "And excuse me if it's too personal. I just wanna know for my own personal reasons."

"Ask away."

Reese didn't ask right away. He didn't know if it was because Tirzah had her sister with her or because of the attitude she was giving him, but he was nervous about asking her the question. He might have lost the courage to ask her at all had Tamera's smartphone not rang at that very moment.

"It's Momma," Tamera said as she got up and walked over toward the door to answer the call.

Reese took a deep breath, settling his nerves, and got ready to ask the question. The amused look on Tirzah's face made him think that perhaps she already knew what was going to come out of his mouth.

"I, uh...was just wondering," he said.

"Wondering what?"

"If...you know."

"Umm, no, I really don't know. I'm not a mind reader. You've got to tell me what's going on in your head for me to give a response. It's called communication."

"I know what it's called."

"Well? Ask away. And let me know whether or not I've got the job so I can know where to go from here. I don't want any callbacks. You're the CEO. I'd rather hear it directly from you than from anybody else."

Reese sighed and rolled his chair closer to the desk. He looked Tirzah up and down, admiring her stunning beauty, and then gathered the courage to say what he had to say and said it:

"Are you seeing somebody?"

"Yes."

"Oh. Oh, okay."

"Was that it? Is that what you wanted to ask me?"

Reese nodded.

Rolling her eyes, Tirzah got up and made a beeline for the door.

"You got the job. Be here by seven-thirty tomorrow night," Reese said, ogling Tirzah and Tamera's thick back-sides as they left his office.

"Damn, joe," Chubb said. "You need to get both of them up in here. You'll definitely make a killing if you did."

"I'ma fuck Tirzah, nigga." Reese kicked his feet up on the desk and nodded his head thoughtfully as he envisioned her on top of him. "She gotta gimme that pussy. I'll pay for it if I got to."

King Rio

Chapter 13

Ciara told them everything she'd been through since leaving Chicago. By the end of her story, Maria was in tears and Jah was holding Ciara tight against his side, stroking her shoulder.

As soon as it looked safe enough to leave, Rell said his goodbyes and urged Jah outside ahead of him. Not once during Ciara's long spiel about how horrible life had been treating her lately did Rell move closer to her. Though it hurt him to see his ex in so much emotional pain, he knew better than to get too close to her. Even if he didn't do anything with her, the scent of her perfume could rub off on him. And what if she hugged him and it went further than just a simple hug and he couldn't stop himself from doing something that he would undoubtedly regret later on? He was buzzing a little off the Remy Martin he'd drank at Shanita's house and he was high and Ciara looked a hundred times better than she used to. He had a feeling that things would take a bad turn if he got too close to Ciara and that was a scenario that he wanted to avoid.

He was doing whatever he could to stay on Tamera's good side.

As it turned out, he would not be so lucky.

Wiping the tears from her face with a Kleenex tissue, Ciara trailed him out the door and asked for a ride.

He turned to her. "A ride to where?"

"To Tops and Bottoms. I need to get a few outfits. Told you my boyfriend stole all my shit. I just talked Capone out of a few hundred to get me some clothes. You know my auntie ain't got no car right now."

Jah chuckled twice as he skipped his way down the stairs.

Rell clamped his teeth together and thought of how mean he would look if he turned her down. He looked back at Jah, then turned and walked closer to Ciara.

"Listen," he said, his voice barely an octave above a whisper, "I'm engaged, a'ight? I know you already knew that, but I'm just saying. No funny stuff. I don't cheat."

"Hmm. That's a surprise to me. Your ass sure didn't mind cheating on me with that thot Erica."

"That was seven years ago."

"Times change; men don't."

"That's a bullshit-ass saying."

"No, it ain't. It's actually the truth. I've learned that if I ain't learned nothing else."

"Whatever." Rell started down the stairs. "Come on. You gon' have to catch a cab back. I'll give you cab fare. Me and lil bruh on one."

Ciara sucked her teeth and rolled her eyes. She followed him to the car and got in behind him as he got in the driver's seat.

The wheels on the Benz had barely began to roll when Ciara continued her rant about Rell cheating on her with Erica.

"What made you cheat on me with that bitch? I mean, of all the hoes we got out here you picked the ugliest, nastiest, most trifling hoe out the bunch."

"I know, right?" Jah said with a laugh.

Rell flipped his little brother a middle finger and kept driving.

"I'm waiting on an answer," Ciara said.

"Keep it up and you gon' be on the next corner waiting for a bus."

"That's so fucked up, Rell. I gave you my fucking virginity. You promised that we would be married by the time we turned twenty-six. What happened to all that shit? Huh? What happened to all those promises?"

Jah nodded his head in agreement with Ciara. Rell briefly considered punching Jah in the face.

"And now you done went and got engaged on me," Ciara went on. "That's so fucked up. Agh, I could slap you right now. I came from Kansas thinking that I would be able to catch up with my old boo and try to see where it would take me but nooooo, your ass is getting married. You should drop a mixtape and name that bitch *Finally Faithful*. Since you done all of a sudden turned into such a good fucking man."

This brought a burst of laughter out of Jah that lasted for almost a full minute.

"We're grown now, Cee. You can't bring up some shit I did when I was sixteen. I just turned twenty-three. I'm a grown-ass man now, and you're a grown woman. Men are a lot different from boys. You should know that by now if you've learned as much as you say you have."

"I learned not to trust no nigga. I know that damn much. I learned that all you muthafuckas are dogs and ain't no sense in looking for nothing more than a nut from your asses. And you wanna know what else I learnt?"

"I really don't, but I'm sure you gon' tell me anyway."

"You're damn right I'ma tell you. I also learned that all you niggas will eventually cheat on a bitch. It's in your genes or something. Like, right now you're all caught up in your feelings for that girl, but I guarantee that within the next few days you gon' come looking for me to fuck, and guess what? I ain't gon' wanna hear it. I'ma ignore your ass and tell you to go and fuck your fiancée."

Rell shook his head. "Whatever, Cee."

"Oh, it's whatever, huh? So if I wanted some dick from you, I couldn't get it? Under no circumstances?"

"I'm done with this conversation," Rell said, and he meant it.

He turned on some music and skipped straight to Lil Wayne's *No Ceilings 2* mixtape, then turned it up full blast and tried to focus on what he and Jah were going to be on once they dropped off Ciara.

Just thinking of it reminded him to take the gun out of his hoodie pocket and slide the long clip back in.

He knew that Jah could not wait to catch the man who'd raped Tirzah.

"Man, fuck them niggas, they hurtin'
She deep throat like a serpent
I stole out too many purses, got too many bitches flirtin'
It's No Ceilings 2, curtains..."

Rell almost elbowed Ciara when she reached in between the seats and cut off the music.

"Never mind on taking me to Tops and Bottoms. Just take me back home to your momma's house. I'll have her take me. I don't like the way you're treating me."

Rell furrowed his brows and looked at her in the rearview mirror. Then he looked at Jah to make sure he wasn't tripping. Jah's chuckle confirmed that Rell was not at all tripping.

Rell had just passed Garfield Park. He was on Madison Street, literally two blocks from the clothing store.

"Fuck that," he said. "I'm letting your ass out at this store and you can go and do you. You got me fucked up if you think I'm about to turn around and go all the way back to my momma's house."

"I'm not getting out of this car, Rell."

"Oh, you gon' get out. One way or the other, you gon' get the fuck up out of here. I don't know what kinda niggas you got used to dealing with in Kansas, but you are back in Chicago, Illinois. Shit don't go how you want it to go when you're in another nigga's car."

She sucked her teeth. "You think you're the shit now 'cause you got some money. Nigga, fuck you and this Benz."

Rell was pulling over in front of Tops and Bottoms, getting ready to physically remove Ciara from the backseat if it came to it, when Jah grabbed his shoulder.

"Look, bruh. That's him. That's the green Jaguar right there. That's Tremaine."

Jah was looking in his side view mirror.

Rell turned in his seat and looked out the rear window. Tremaine's green Jaguar was parked outside the MetroPCS store right next to Tops and Bottoms, and Tremaine was in the driver's seat.

There was a young woman in a yellow coat walking out of the MetroPCS store. Tremaine's eyes were on her. He leaned over and opened the door for her, and she got in and gave him a kiss before shutting the door.

"Cee, you gotta get out," Rell said as he watched Tremaine pull off.

Ciara crossed her arms belligerently. "I said I'm not getting out."

"Bruh, follow that nigga!" Jah snapped.

Tremaine didn't even look their way as he drove around the Benz and passed them.

Rell pulled off, a bit irritated with Ciara for not getting out of the car, but too focused on the Jaguar to give it much thought.

"Whatever you do," Rell said to Jah, "don't start shooting right here on Madison. Too many witnesses. We'll follow him until we're somewhere on a side street."

Jah had the Mac-10 gripped tight in his hands. His eyes were locked on Tremaine's car.

"Bruh, you heard what I said?"

"Yeah, man." Jah nodded once.

The Jaguar made a left turn at the corner and then a quick right into the Church's restaurant's parking lot.

Rell followed it into the parking lot and stopped in the next row from where Tremaine parked.

"Should just chop up his punk ass right here," Jah said.

"No the fuck you shouldn't." Rell glanced over at Jah. "Nigga, this car is rented in my name. We ain't on no dumb shit. Just chill out and wait."

Ciara said, "Oh, my God, are y'all about to shoot this nigga? What did he do?"

"This is exactly why I didn't want you in the car with us," Rell said.

"Oh, please. I've seen niggas get shot before. Shit, I just saw Capone shoot that boy. Stop acting like I didn't run the streets with you back in the day. I am from Chicago, nigga. Chi-mothafuckin-Raq. I ain't new to this. I'm true to this."

"If you don't shut the fuck up with that bullshit, Cee. Be quiet and shut up."

"That's the same thing. Quiet and shut up. Genius."

Rell didn't respond to her smart-mouthed remark. He realized that he'd misspoken. He had a good excuse. His adrenaline was pumping. He was mere feet from the man who'd raped his fiancée's sister yesterday. He wanted to do something. Something bad. Something serious.

He sat behind the wheel and watched as Tremaine and the girl in the yellow coat got out of the Jaguar and entered the restaurant.

With nothing else to do here in the presence of so many possible eyewitnesses, he and Jah had no choice but to wait.

Which is exactly what they did.

Chapter 14

"This that James pack right here, big bruh. Haaaaa! You see how I wet that nigga up? Thought he was gon' just slide through D Block and fuck one of our hoes without gettin' hit up? Fuck was he thinkin'?" Capone said, inhaling a puff of Blue Dream Kush smoke and blowing it out in rings.

He was in the passenger seat of the light gray Altima he and Johnny B had just purchased for $9,000 from a local used car lot. He had put $3,000 on the car and Johnny B said that they would take turns using the car until Johnny B paid him the $3,000 back.

They were driving aimlessly around the North Lawndale neighborhood, smoking blunts and listening to drill music while simultaneously keeping their eyes peeled for opps. In this case, their opps were members of the same branch of Vice Lord that they were members of, just a different set. Their opps were the TVLs in Zo's clique.

"You did give it to that nigga," Johnny B said, coughing on the Kush smoke. "But look, though, I might have a lil thot for us over here on Douglas. She just moved into bro n'em building a few days ago. Bad lil bitch, too. Skinny as fuck, but on Neal, she's bad. We might be able to run this bitch."

"Say no more. I'm all the way in, big homie. Let's slide."

Nodding his head, Johnny B turned off 16th Street and onto Homan Avenue. He paid attention to every single person on the sidewalk and every single vehicle on the street. "No lacking" was the motto in Chiraq, and he was not planning on losing his life any time soon. He had a Ruger pistol on his lap with a 30-shot clip. Capone's 9 millimeter held a 16-round magazine and was also equipped with red laser sighting.

Both of them had rounds chambered and ready to fire.

Johnny B made it to Rell and Jah's apartment building on the corner of Douglas and Homan without incident. He parked behind a raggedy red Ford Taurus and they got out with their guns on their hips, eyes low and as red as the Taurus from the Kush.

"I hope this bitch got some food in this mu'fucka," Capone said, rubbing his belly as they climbed the stairs.

He was excited to be out and about with Johnny B. He had always wanted to kick it with the tall, Jamaican-looking shooter. It was Johnny B who'd inspired Capone to grow out his dreadlocks in the first place. He looked up to Johnny B in the same way that most of their squad looked up to Jah. He remembered being at a girl named Tina's birthday party last summer and seeing Johnny B give the biggest guy in the house a vicious knockout punch for rubbing up on the wrong girl. The guy had later returned and shot up the party, wounding three people and killing the birthday girl, but what stuck with Capone most about that night was how quickly Johnny B had swung on the big guy. Since then, Capone had gotten into a number of fights at school — which is why he was now expelled — and each time he'd taken on his opponent with the same braveness he'd seen in Johnny B that night.

They went to an apartment on the first floor of the building and Johnny B knocked on the door.

"Let me do all the talking," Johnny B whispered.

Capone nodded his head. He would keep his mouth shut and let Johnny B do the talking.

A girl's voice sounded from the other side of the door.

"Who is it?"

"It's me. Johnny B."

Capone thought it was cool how Johnny B's name sounded just then.

The door opened, and there stood a light-skinned girl with short red hair. She had on a pair of Minnie Mouse pajama pants and a T-shirt.

She waved for them to come in and told Johnny B to lock the door behind him as she headed to a spot on the dingy blue sofa, where she had obviously been sitting when Johnny B knocked on her door. She wrapped herself up in a tan-colored blanket and shivered.

"That heat ain't working too good," she said. "It's colder than a motherfucker in here."

Johnny B suggested that she put on a sweatshirt, but she shook her head and didn't answer.

He sat down next to her and got under the blanket with her while Capone took a chair from the kitchen and sat down on it.

The television was on. The girl was watching *Family Guy*, one of Capone's favorite TV shows.

He sat there and watched the show while Johnny B whispered in the girl's ear. The blanket began moving and Capone suspected that Johnny B was playing in the girl's pussy. Just thinking about it made Capone's dick get hard. He pressed it down against his inner thigh, not wanting to embarrass himself in front of the girl.

Seconds later, Johnny B and the girl got up with the blanket wrapped around them and left Capone alone in the living room.

"Man, I hope bro ain't just gon' leave me sitting here like this," Capone said aloud to himself as he dialed Jah's number on his smartphone.

"What up, lil homie?" Jah answered.

"Shit, man. I just wanted to say thanks for the money earlier. Me and bro done got us a car and everything. A brand-new Altima. We at this thot's crib right now in y'all building on Douglas. I'm hoping bro don't fuck around and leave me out the play."

"I hate to cut you off, lil homie," Jah said, "but on Neal, this ain't the time to talk. I'm staked out on a nigga right now. Lemme hit you back in a lil while."

"Aw, okay. Yup, yup, just hit me up later."

"Solid, lil bruh," Jah said.

"Solid."

Just as Capone was slipping the phone in his pocket, Johnny B shouted for him to come and join them in the bedroom.

Capone stood up and took a deep breath. He was nervous, just as he always was when he was around a girl that he might be close to fucking.

When he walked in the bedroom, the girl was sucking Johnny B's dick under the blanket.

"Come in and close the door," Johnny B said, and Capone followed the big homie's orders, though he couldn't understand why he had to shut the door when the three of them were the only people in the apartment.

"Get back there and hit that shit," Johnny B said. "Unless you want her to knock you off to get yo' shit hard."

Capone shook his head. He didn't need the girl to suck on his dick to get it hard. His dick was already hard.

He lifted the blanket and unzipped his jeans at the same time. The girl's pajama bottoms were already down to her knees. Capone didn't have a condom but he didn't care and evidently she didn't care, either, because she didn't say a word as he pushed the head of his dick in her pussy and put his hands on her bony hips.

He eased into her. She was tight and wet. Her pussy was nice and warm. He stared down at his dick and saw her creamy juices stretching across his length as he sank deeper and deeper into her. She moaned lightly as he quickened in speed. Her head bounced like crazy under the blanket.

"D Block, nigga," Johnny B said, smiling at Capone and making the T with his hands that represented their gang.

Capone returned the smile and the T and said, "D Block for life, nigga. Fuck the other side."

Biting down on his lower lip, Capone looked down at the girl's exposed bottom and realized that he didn't even know her name. Wasn't like it mattered, though. All that really mattered was the nut he was about to get out of it.

They stayed in the same position until, just five minutes later, Capone pulled out and shot off a few drops of cum on her lower back.

He was getting to his feet and pulling his pants up when Johnny B clamped his hands on the girl's head and came in her mouth. She choked and gagged and coughed as he filled her throat with cum, but she kept at it until he was done.

Johnny B said a couple of words and then he waved for Capone to follow him and they left the apartment as quickly as they had come.

Capone was all smiles. This time Johnny B let him drive. He sped off down Douglas feeling like a boss.

"Slow down, lil homie. Can't get pulled over with these poles on us. Stop at Anna's so we can grab another cigar," Johnny B said. "Then I gotta stop by my auntie's crib right around the corner from Anna's. You can drop me off and do you after that. Just don't fuck up the car."

"If you think I'ma fuck this up, you don't know me, big homie. We need this whip to slide on niggas when they get outta line, and to slide down on thots like lil momma we just busted down. What was her name?"

Johnny B shrugged. "Something with a Q. Quita or Qui-ana, some shit like that. I really don't even know, to tell you the truth. You should've asked her."

Capone laughed at the fact that neither he nor Johnny B knew the girl's name after having been so intimate with her just moments prior. He pulled up at Anna's, the convenience store on 13th and Kedzie, and waited in the car while Johnny B went inside.

Knowing how worried his mom, Chrissy, always got when his hood was warring with another block, he gave her a call while he waited.

She sounded relieved when she answered. "Boy, I was so worried," she said. "I heard some boy got killed on Erica's front porch over there on 13th and Avers and the first person I thought of was you."

Capone laughed, adjusting his seat to his liking. "You ain't gotta worry about me, Ma. You know I got this."

"You coming over for dinner?"

"On my way in about twenty minutes."

"Okay, be safe out there, you hear me? I love you, baby."

Capone chuckled. "Love you, too, Ma."

He was just ending the call when Johnny B got back in the car.

He turned onto 13th Street and Johnny B showed him where to stop. Johnny B's aunt lived in an upstairs apartment on Troy. They got out of the car together and headed alongside the house, which is where Capone's body was found twenty minutes later with two bullet wounds to the back of his head.

Chapter 15

"Bitch, I am dead. Look at this crazy bitch Cardi B," Tirzah said, laughing hysterically as she watched a video of the Instagram star on her iPad.

She and Tamera had returned home from Redbone's and were sitting Indian style on the living room sofa, scrolling through Instagram on their iPad computer tablets and drinking cups of hot cocoa. They had changed out of their clothes and were now wearing matching Minions pajamas.

"Don't know why we're drinking hot chocolate when we know that Tara's on her way over with Remy," Tamera said once they were done laughing at Cardi B. "It's time to turn up and we're sitting here drinking hot cocoa like some lames."

"We are some lames."

"Speak for yourself. I ain't no lame."

"Nigga," Tirzah said, "you are about to get married at the age of twenty-two. It doesn't get any lamer than that. Sorry to break it to you."

"And? You're twenty-six. What's the difference?"

"Four years is a long time. That's a long difference. You haven't even really lived yet."

"Yeah, and neither has the boy you're about to marry."

Tirzah cut a glance at Tamera. "I caught that shade, hoe."

Tamera laughed and sipped her hot cocoa, which made Tirzah bust out laughing again.

"Kermit-looking bitch, I can't stand you." Tirzah put down the iPad and struggled to put on a serious face. "Listen, though. I want your honest to God opinion."

"My opinion on what?"

"Me working at the club? Do you think I should go through with it?"

Tamera shrugged. "You're a grown woman. Without a job, I might add. I thought about that earlier. You're right. If Rell put me out today all I have to fall back on is the twenty-five grand I saved from that money I took from Shalonda. That's a lot more than I had when we were living together, but it's not enough to live on. I don't know. Maybe I should go and work there, too."

"No. You're set. Rell's mature. It's Jah who's mentally unbalanced. If he broke up with me yesterday, I can't expect him not to do it again, and I gotta be ready."

"What about the wedding?" Tamera asked as she set down her cup on a coaster and stretched out her legs. "I'm just asking because I'm planning to get married this summer, maybe even sooner. I really don't even wanna wait that long. Have you and Jah talked about a date?"

Tirzah shook her head and sighed. "That nigga ain't talked about a damn thing. All he wants to do is fuck and play video games."

Tamera fell over against Tirzah and laughed. Tirzah elbowed Tamera in the arm.

"Shit ain't funny, bitch." Tirzah scowled.

"It really is. He ain't even eighteen yet. You act like you expected him to do something different. There's a remedy to that. All you gotta do is put that pussy on him right and then stop right in the middle of the session and make some demands. Works every time."

Tirzah became thoughtful. She pulled at the string that extended from her pajama shirt. They had gotten Minions pajamas because they both loved the Minions in the *Despicable Me* movies. Tirzah looked at the engagement ring Jah had proposed to her with, so Tamera looked at hers.

The ring on Tamera's finger was a lot more expensive than Tirzah's. It was a beautiful nine-carat diamond ring worth

$100,000. Tamera absolutely loved it. The only thing she loved more than the ring was not a thing at all. It was a man. Sincere Jerrell Owens. Without him the ring meant nothing.

"Reese wants me, sis," Tirzah said. "Did you see the way he was staring at me? He was practically drooling. And he's rich. Filthy rich. Fuck."

"Why'd you say it like that?"

"Because he had to wait for me to get engaged to try and holler. His smart ass could've hollered a long time ago."

"Are you saying you want to be with him instead of Jah?"

"No, I'm not saying that. What I'm saying is...you know what the hell I'm saying. Reese is the richest nigga out here. Everybody wants that nigga. Look at his damn nickname. They don't call him Bankroll Reese for nothing. That's Cup Junior, you know what I'm saying? He's the most wanted man alive on the west side. I can't help but think I might have made a mistake. Maybe I should've messed around with Reese. Just think if I had a baby by him. I'd be rich. I'd be able to pay my own bills just off child support alone."

"You shouldn't think like that, Tirz. There is more to life than money. You've got love. Real love. True love. Jah might be young, but he's a real nigga. You don't know what kinda nigga Reese is. All you know is that he got some money. I'd rather be homeless with Rell than to be rich with either of my exes, and that's the whole truth and nothing but the truth."

"Yeah, you say that shit now. You didn't just have a mul-timillionaire drooling over you."

"I don't give a damn what he was doing. I love Rell and only Rell."

"Yeah, well, Rell didn't break up with you on Valentine's Day to spend some time with his baby's momma. That shit hurt me, Tamera. I'm serious. Maybe Jah needs a taste of his own medicine. I should let Reese take me out on a date or some shit, just for the heck of it. Let Jah see how it feels to be hurt like that."

"You're being foolish, Tirzah."

"No, I'm not being foolish. I'm being real. I'm being honest."

"Whatever." Tamera shook her head and rolled her eyes at Tirzah's stupidity. "You need to have a talk with Jah if you feel like that. Y'all might wanna call off the engagement."

As if on cue, Tirzah's smartphone began ringing at that very moment with a call from Jah. She leaned forward and picked up the phone off the coffee table.

Tamera heard Jah say, "Come outside to the backyard. We got that nigga."

Chapter 16

They had followed the Jaguar for more than twenty minutes after leaving Church's before they were finally able to catch Tremaine on a side street as he was sitting in the car waiting on the girl in the yellow coat to come back out of the house she had just entered.

It happened quickly.

Jah had just about ripped off the Jaguar's driver's door as he snatched Tremaine out of it, and after he and Rell gave Tremaine a good beating with their gloved fists and guns, they put him in his own trunk and Jah drove it to the house on Trumbull while Rell trailed behind in the Benz, stopping just once to drop off Ciara, who suddenly had no problem with getting out of the Benz.

Jah parked the Jaguar in the garage and waited for Rell to join him before he opened the trunk.

"Yeah, nigga. Wake up," Jah said, roughly shoving the barrel of his gun against the back of Tremaine's head.

Tremaine wasn't sleeping. He probably wished he could be asleep, but he definitely was not sleeping. His head was swollen and bloodied. There was blood all over his gray leather jacket, and Jah was dragging him out of the trunk by its collar when the girls walked in through the garage's side door.

"You wanna rape women?" Rell said, taking down a shovel that was hanging on the wall. He swung it as hard as he could at Tremaine's head and enjoyed the wonderful "ding" sound it made as it struck the older man.

Tremaine groaned and fell to his hands and knees, blood dripping from his head and face, his arms trembling fiercely.

Rell looked at Tirzah as she took a crowbar off the top of his tool chest and slammed it down on Tremaine's back. He collapsed onto his stomach and let out a scream.

"Well, well, well," Tirzah said, slowly nodding her head as her eyes remained unwaveringly glued to Tremaine. "Christmas came early this year for a real bitch. You motherfucker!" She hit him across the back again. "You fucking raped me! You motherfucker, you raped me! You fucking raped me!"

The crowbar clinked onto the cold concrete floor as Tirzah dropped it. She curled her fingers into the waistline of Tremaine's slacks and pulled and pulled until they slid down to his knees.

"I'm sorry, man," Tremaine said weakly. "Just...let me...just let me go. Just let me go home to my momma...my kids."

"Oh, no. Hell no!" Tirzah picked up the crowbar and repeatedly slammed it across his bare legs. He twitched and jerked around on the ground. Jah and Rell pulled Tamera back so that Tirzah could take out all her frustrations on Tremaine and get the revenge she deserved. He had raped her yesterday. In Rell's opinion, he deserved every ounce of physical pain he was feeling.

The garage had been redone shortly before Rell and Jah's father bought the house for them. The concrete floor was perfectly smooth, and there were tools for every occasion hanging on the walls and in the tool chest.

Seeing Tirzah standing over Tremaine in her heavy leather Pelle Pelle jacket, Minions pajamas, and UGG boots might have been funny if she were not assaulting Tremaine with a crowbar. He screamed and howled like a wounded animal but Tirzah did not let up, not even when he went unconscious from enduring all the pain. She beat his hairy legs to a bloody pulp. She kicked him over onto his back and beat his chest until the crow bar started sinking in through the broken bones of his ribcage. Then she mutilated his dick with the jagged tip of the crow bar, which is when Tamera and Jah had to turn their heads and shut their eyes.

But Rell watched. He watched because he thought that Tremaine was a sick individual for raping a woman. He watched because Tirzah was sobbing as she assaulted Tremaine and he knew that her anger at having been raped by the cowardly man had taken over her senses. She was in a rage, and she had a right to be that way. No one could blame her for it.

"Okay, okay," Tamera said, head still turned, eyes still shut. "Somebody stop her. That's enough."

Rell walked up behind Tirzah and grabbed ahold of her right wrist, then took the crow bar from her and held her as she fell against his chest and cried. He walked her over to where Tamera was standing and Tamera joined in on the consoling hug.

"Baby, take her in the house," Rell said to Tamera. "Make her take off those pajamas and boots and that jacket and put 'em all in one trash bag. I'll go and buy her some new ones."

Tamera left out the garage's side door with Tirzah's head on her shoulder. Rell waited until they were on the back porch before he turned to Jah and spoke.

"The fuck we gon' do with this nigga, lil bruh?"

Jah shrugged, squinting at Tremaine's body as they walked closer to it.

"Is he dead?" Jah asked.

"Fuck if I know. Put your head on his chest and listen for a heartbeat."

"You got me too fucked up." Jah squatted down on his haunches and studied Tremaine's horribly beaten body. "Damn, bruh. She fucked this nigga up, joe. Bad! Damn. Look at his dick! Ughhh."

"That's what the fuck he get. Ol' bitch-ass nigga wanna rape a woman. He got what he deserved, you ask me."

"I would've just shot the nigga, bruh. Damn. This shit is ugly. And she didn't hit him in the face not one time. She wanted his ass to suffer. If he is alive, he ain't gon' be raping nobody else. Not no time soon."

It was true. Tremaine's dick was halfway severed, and it looked like all of his ribs were broken.

"Get his feet, bruh," Rell said.

He grabbed Tremaine's hands and Jah got the battered man's feet. They lifted him from the bloody floor and tossed him back into the trunk of the Jaguar.

"We might as well just pop this nigga, bruh," Jah suggested. "Ain't no sense in leaving him alive. Fuck it. I wanna whack him for raping baby, anyway. Plus, he saw our faces. And what if somebody else over there saw us. We can't let him live. No face, no case. You know the rules."

Rell slammed the trunk shut and nodded his head. "I feel you, but at the same time, I don't. We don't need to make the block no hotter than it already is. And you gotta think of the emotional pain that rape put on Tirz. Let this nigga live if he can. He'll be in way more pain than she's in, I can guarantee you that much."

"So, what we supposed to do with the car?"

Rell shrugged his shoulders. "Drop it off in an alley somewhere and leave the trunk open. Somebody will eventually find him."

"One down, one more to go. Now all we need to do is get that nigga Zo and put him in a trunk. Then we can go ahead and get married and leave all this bullshit to the streets."

"I hope so," Rell said just as his iPhone vibrated on his hip.

It was a text message from Lil Larry:

"Bro dey just found Capone dead on 13th bro on neal I'm too sick"

King Rio

Chapter 17

Zo was distraught over his brother's death, but the text message he'd just gotten from Johnny B put a smile on his face. A brief smile, a smile that lasted just ten seconds or so, but a smile nonetheless.

The guy who had killed James was dead.

Standing in the alley behind his big sister's house, with his cold hands stuffed in the pockets of his white leather jacket, Zo had his chin lowered to his chest to keep the frigid air from hitting his neck.

Zaniyah and her friend Lisa were beside him, and there were over thirty more people in the alley with them. They were smoking blunts of potent marijuana, provided by Zo. Some were drinking cups of cognac, and others were drinking cups of vodka. A few of them were crying silently over Roddy's death.

But not Zo. Zo was done crying. Zo was ready to get some payback.

He had shot Felicia, but that wasn't enough. He wanted to do some real damage to Jah and Rell.

He couldn't wait for Johnny B to finally get it done.

"Bae, it is too fucking cold out here," Zaniyah said as she got behind him and wrapped her arms around his waist. "We need to go inside. We can all go to my house. I don't want all these niggas in my shit, but damn, I'd rather be in the house than out here."

Zo nodded his head. He told everyone that he'd be back in a few minutes and then walked off with Zaniyah's arms still wrapped around him.

Lisa fell in step next to him, texting on her smartphone as they walked alongside Odella's house to Homan Avenue. "I don't know if y'all heard or not, but they say one of them

D Block niggas just got hit up over there on 13th. At least we ain't the only ones taking losses, you know what I'm saying? We lost E, Chris, and Roddy. It's about time they started losing some niggas, too."

"Who was it that got killed on 13th?" Zaniyah asked.

Lisa shrugged. "Some nigga named Capone. I don't know who he is. They say he's a lot younger than us. He was fourteen or fifteen. Something like that. Whoever did it shot him in the head."

They crossed Homan and rushed into Zaniyah's house, stomping the snow off their shoes as they walked in.

Zo went straight to the stove and held his hands over the fire to warm them. His nose and lips were numb from the cold. Seconds later, Zaniyah and Lisa were bunched around the stove with him.

"Our cold asses," Zaniyah said with a laugh. "Shit. It must be below 0 out there. I'm half-drunk and still cold as fuck."

Zo lit a cigarette on the flames and sat down at the small square kitchen table. His mind was running a mile a minute. He hoped that Johnny B would get away with killing Capone, if only until he got the chance to do Jah the same way. As long as Jah got it in the end, Zo didn't give a damn how everything else played out.

"Y'all wanna get in the bed and cuddle with each other for a few minutes?" Zaniyah said, looking from Lisa to Zo. "Just to warm up." She laughed. "I ain't on no freaky shit."

Zo shook his head. "Nah, I'm good," he said, but when Zaniyah and Lisa headed upstairs he followed them and once they took off their jackets and shoes, he ended up right between them in the bed.

It felt a hundred percent better under the covers than it did outside in the cold. Zaniyah put her head on his right shoulder, so Lisa followed suit and put hers on his other shoulder. Lisa was a lot heavier than Zaniyah and just as beautiful. Zo had known both of them since grade school.

They lay together for a while, watching Lisa text her friend about Capone's murder. Nobody had a clue who'd done it, but of course, half the neighborhood suspected that Zo's gang had something to do with it. Everybody knew that Zo and Jah were beefing, which meant that Zo's squad and Jah's squad were also at each other's heads.

He wondered what would happen if the truth ever got out about what really had happened to Capone.

Zaniyah got up and turned on some music. She was one of the few people in the hood who still bought CDs from the store instead of getting them bootleg from the street hustlers. She put Drake's old *Take Care* album in her PlayStation 3 and hit play.

When she got back in the bed next to Zo, she and Lisa began texting each other back and forth. He looked at one text on Lisa's phone that said "Just do it right now he won't say shit" and he almost knew what was coming next.

Lisa set aside her smartphone and lifted the covers over her head as she slipped beneath them. Zaniyah started kissing Zo's face and neck and rubbing on his chest just as Lisa's cool hands pulled his dick out of his boxers.

He could tell right away what kind of head he was about to get. Lisa was one of those girls who only sucked on the head while stroking the rest of the dick in her hands, and she salivated a lot, which made for a pretty wet time.

Zo didn't care how she sucked dick. Just a couple of months ago, when he was dead broke and as filthy as they come, she would not have sucked his dick to save her own life. Now that he was getting money, Lisa — like most of the girls in the hood — could not wait to get a taste of his dick.

Zaniyah must have read his mind. She put her mouth next to his ear and said, "I know you probably look at a lot of us like, 'Why the fuck you like me now? You never liked me before.' But that's not the case at all. We liked you, but we didn't see the potential you had to be a man. Real men get money, and you've shown us all just how real you are."

"Money don't make a nigga real," Zo said. "I know plenty of broke real niggas and plenty of niggas with bread who ain't standing on shit. It's what's in a nigga's heart that makes 'em real. It's how a nigga reacts to certain situations out here in these streets. If I would've went to the law about Jah, I would be a fake-ass nigga, no matter if I had a million dollars at the time. Real is just in a mu'fucka. Money ain't got shit to do with it."

Zaniyah shrugged and planted a kiss on his shoulder. "Well, it must have took you getting money for us to recognize how real you are. Whatever the case, we see it now. We definitely see it now."

I just bet you do, Zo thought to himself as Zaniyah pulled back the covers and went down to join Lisa.

Drake's "Take Care" sounded good on top of the sucking sounds of Zaniyah and Lisa's mouths. Zo fired up a cigarette and took a puff and listened:

"When all the baggage just ain't as heavy and the party's over, just don't forget me
We'll change the pace and we'll just go slow.
You won't ever have to worry, you won't ever have to hide.
You've seen all my mistakes, so look me in my eyes..."

Although Drake had not been among Zo's list of rappers to listen to ever since the Canadian lyricist's infamous Meek

112

Mill diss, he listened to the song and enjoyed it for the first time. It was an old song that he'd never heard all the way through. Once he heard Rihanna's sweet voice at the beginning, he was all ears.

He watched Zaniyah and Lisa do their thing. Lisa was sucking on his balls, and Zaniyah's lips were bobbing up and down on his shaft. The two of them weren't the best of dick-suckers, but they got the job done. They weren't like Keyonna, the girl who lived around the corner on Christiana. Keyonna had sucked Zo's dick for about two hours the other day, and she'd been so bad at it that he had not ejaculated until he jerked himself off on her face. Having experienced such an inexperienced blowjob made Zo appreciate the rookie attempt that Zaniyah and Lisa were making to please him. He didn't mind that it wasn't the best head in the world. At a stressful time like this, he needed all the relaxation he could get.

"...It's my birthday, I'll get high if I want to
Can't deny that I want you, but I'll lie if I have to
'Cause you don't say you love me to your friends when they ask you
Even though we both know that you do...you do..."

Zaniyah looked up at Zo and kept her eyes on him as he tensed up and gasped. He lifted his sweatshirt out of the way as a copious load of semen spewed out of him. As usual, Zaniyah seemed afraid of his cum, refusing to even let her tongue touch it, but Lisa wasn't afraid of it. She sucked the rest of it out of his dick and then licked up the large amount that had spurted on to his abdomen.

He got up to go and clean himself off in the bathroom, but he had only made it to the bedroom door when the sound of gunfire sent him ducking for cover.

King Rio

Chapter 18

Rell and Jah ducked low in the Jaguar's front seats, and Rell stomped down on the gas pedal as bullets pierced the luxury car's exterior.

Holes appeared in the windows. The front driver's side tire flattened, and suddenly sparks were flying from it.

Fearing for his life, Rell kept his head down as he veered around the corner onto 15th Street, shouting for Jah to start shooting back.

Jah raised the fully-automatic Mac-10 and opened fire on the guys who were chasing behind the Jaguar on foot. Rell glanced at his side view mirror and saw that the spray of gunfire grounded one of the guys and sent the rest scattering.

"Bitch-ass niggas!" Jah shouted, growing more courageous as he emptied the clip at their enemies.

The plan had gone wrong as soon as Rell turned onto Spaulding Avenue.

He and Jah had intended to ditch Tremaine's car somewhere on Zo's block and then head back home to Tamera and Tirzah, not expecting to run into what seemed like every single one of Zo's guys in the process.

He lost control of the Jaguar on Sawyer and crashed into a parked car.

Jah hit his head on the windshield, but he was okay. He grabbed the shoulder of Rell's jacket and shouted for him to come on.

As they got out of the car, Rell drawing his Glock pistol, Jah loading another 50-round clip into the Mac, they noticed a rapidly-approaching pair of headlights coming right at them. A guy stuck his upper body out of the passenger's window and aimed an assault rifle at Rell and Jah.

Heart pounding, Rell quickly took aim and opened fire just as the assault rifle started blasting, praying that his bullets hit the shooter before the shooter's high-caliber rounds hit him.

Jah opened up on the approaching vehicle with the Mac-10.

Luckily, the assault rifle that was firing at them was not a fully-automatic weapon like Jah's submachine gun. It hardly got off seven or eight shots before the car's windshield was completely riddled with bullet holes.

The car veered off the street, barreled through a vacant lot, and collided head on with an iron fence in the alley on Sawyer.

An older man who'd been walking down 15th with his young daughter had pushed her to the ground and laid over her. Now, he got up, picking her up with him, and ran towards Kedzie.

"Look, bruh! It's Ms. Williams!" Jah said, pointing ahead of them at the small red Ford coupe that was just pulling off from the apartment building on 15th and Kedzie.

Monica Williams was an old friend of their mother's.

Rell and Jah tucked away their guns and shouted for her. She looked at them with frightened eyes as they ran up to her car, then sighed and put a hand on her chest when she realized that it was them.

"We need a ride, Ms. Williams. These niggas out here shooting," Jah said, not even bothering to wait and see if she would agree to drive them anywhere as he snatched open the door behind her and got in.

Rell got in next to Jah.

"I got a hundred for you. Just take us to my momma's house."

Ms. Williams, usually a slow driver, sped off so fast that the Ford's tires screeched.

Rell looked over his shoulder until Ms. Williams turned down Douglas Boulevard and headed toward Maria's house.

"Jesus H. Christ. What in God's name is going on?" Ms. Williams asked, still holding a hand to her chest.

Rell had no answer for her so he kept quiet.

She went on. "I just talked to Maria 'bout this last time she showed her face at church. The end is near. The world is going to hell in a handbag. I've lived here in Chicago my whole life. Never has it been as bad as it is now. I don't know what's changed but it's definitely something. I think it's the devil. Satan's getting stronger and stronger. You can see the signs everywhere. Jesus is coming. You'd better believe that if you don't believe anything else. Jesus is coming and he is coming soon. All we can do is prepare for it and..."

Rell tuned out the old lady's religious rant and phoned Tamera to let her know what had just happened.

It sounded like Tamera was crying. Tirzah was crying in the background.

"You big-ass crybabies," Rell said.

"Shut up." Tamera sniffled and blew her nose. "Facetime me. We never use it anymore. I wanna see you."

"I'm on my way to Momma's house. I'll Facetime you soon's we get there."

"Did you hear all those shots? Somebody's shooting somewhere around here. It sounded close."

"That's because it was me they were shooting at."

"Really? Who was it? Zo?"

"I'll explain it to you later. Just keep your gun out and ready to shoot. Turn out all the lights. Get the choppa out our bedroom and go downstairs to the basement. I want y'all to stay down there until we make it back home. Okay?"

"No, Rell. It's not fucking okay. There's too much happening right now. I'm gonna have a nervous fucking breakdown."

"If you have a meltdown, who's gonna help me? Who's gonna help Tirzah? How are we gonna get married?"

"Whatever. This shit is driving me nuts, Rell. Fuck. I'm done. I am so fucking done. You don't even understand the level of done I'm on right now. My sister's crying so much that she's got me crying. You're getting shot at and telling me to be ready to shoot somebody tonight. What the fuck, Rell? Didn't I say that we needed to get the fuck away from here? Didn't I just tell you that today? Do you even hear me when I'm talking, or does it just go in one ear and out the fucking other?"

"I know, baby." Rell sighed. He used his teeth to loosen the fingers of his black leather gloves enough to easily take them off. "Okay, just take the suitcase out the closet, get in your car, and go to a hotel room. Have Tirzah drive my rental. We'll get a room and stay there until we find a new place to live. Is that okay? Call Tara and tell her to just meet us at the hotel instead of coming to the house."

"I don't know how much more of this I can take, Rell. I really don't."

"It ain't gon' be no more, baby. It's about me and you from now on. I promise. I'm sorry for putting you through all this shit and I promise that it'll never happen again. Fuck the hood. I'm about to get us a new house as soon as possible. But first we gotta get the fuck away from here and to some place safe."

Tamera paused for a long moment, during which time Rell heard Tirzah's phone ringing in the background. He looked over and saw that it was Jah phoning Tirzah while at the same time looking out the back window to make sure that they weren't being followed.

A police car zipped past.

Monica had yet to stop preaching about the second coming of Jesus.

"Okay," Tamera said finally. "I'm getting my shoes back on now. I'll call and let you know which hotel we go to. Be careful out there, Rell. Please. I can't lose you. You're the best thing that's ever happened to me."

"Don't worry about me, baby. Just get to that hotel and then call me. Me and Jah about to dip these straps off. We'll take Momma's truck to the hotel."

"Okay." Another sniffle from Tamera. "I'll see you in a bit. Love you."

"Love you more," Rell said, and ended the call just as Monica made it to 13th and Avers.

The D Block gang was once again in full effect. They were standing out in front of Momma's house, just a few houses down from where Capone had shot and killed Zo's worker earlier in the day.

It was getting dark out. A couple of the guys reached for their guns until they saw that it was Rell and Jah in Monica's backseat.

"Tell Maria I say we wanna see her face this Sunday at church. She ain't came in God knows how long," Ms. Williams said as Rell handed her a hundred-dollar bill and stepped out of the car.

The tallest member of the D Block gang was Johnny B. He towered over everyone else. Rell immediately spotted him standing among the other guys.

"We out here cappin' for Capone, nigga," Johnny B said, raising a bottle of Remy in Capone's honor. "Fuck niggas took one of the realest young niggas we had. Capone was harder than most these grown niggas. Can't believe this shit, bruh. On Neal, we goin' hard for the lil homie. Soon's we find out who did that shit a nigga gets it."

Rell nodded his head in agreement.

Jah teared up. Capone had been one of his best friends. They'd done a lot together in the past. The pain in Jah's eyes spoke volumes about how much he was hurting on the inside.

Rell decided against telling the gang about what had just gone down on 15th Street, for fear that he and Jah had killed someone in the shooting. There was never any telling who would end up being a snitch later on down the line. He had learned not to make that kind of mistake in prison. Many of his cellmates had only been convicted because of confessions from friends of theirs.

He grabbed the bottle from Johnny B and took a big gulp of the liquor before he and Jah headed in to Momma's house.

As soon as he walked in the door, Momma and Ciara looked up from the sofa and stared at him and Jah, neither of them saying a word.

"What the hell y'all looking at us like that for?" Rell said.

Momma rolled her eyes and turned back to watching an episode of *Scandal* on the television. She spoke without looking at him.

"Running around here snatching people out of their cars, Rell? Putting people in trunks? Have you lost your damn mind?"

Rell's eyes shifted to Ciara, but he didn't say what he wanted to say.

However, Jah was not as good at biting his tongue.

"You lil snitch," Jah said to Ciara, who then rolled her eyes and smiled.

"You don't know what happened, Ma," Rell said, picking up the keys to her SUV off the coffee table. "Ms. Williams said she wanna see you in church this Sunday."

"Tell her she can come and see me in hell this Monday."

Everyone but Momma laughed.

"Put my damn keys down," she said.

"I need you to drop me off at a hotel. I'll pay you."

"I ain't doing no damn drop-offs. Put my keys down. Ask one of your so-called friends. They got money to smoke blunts all day. I know they can afford to drop y'all off."

Rell let out a sigh and shook his head. He was just about to turn and head back out the door when something caught his eye.

There were two suitcases sitting against the wall next to the closet, along with several pairs of women's shoes that were too flashy to belong to Momma. He looked from the shoes to Ciara and then to Momma, squinting, thinking.

"This better not be what I think it is," he said through tightly-clenched teeth.

"What's in my house is my business," Maria said.

Jah laughed and walked to the kitchen, shaking his head and swinging his arms at his sides.

"It won't be for long," Ciara said. "Just until I get my stuff together. I didn't ask. She offered."

"Girl, you ain't gotta explain nothing to nobody about you moving into what's mine. I pay all the bills in here. Every single one of 'em. Always have, even when they stayed here with me."

Furious, Rell stormed off to the bedroom that had been his ever since he was born and started bagging up the few items of clothing he had left here. He didn't like what was going on, but Momma was right. He was a grown-ass man. He had a feeling that Ciara was only staying here to try and get close to him, and if that was the case, then she had already failed. He was all about Tamera and nothing was going to change about that. He didn't care if Beyoncé came to live with Momma. He was leaving for good this time.

He was shoving his things into a backpack when Ciara appeared in his bedroom doorway with her hands on her hips. She leaned against the doorframe and smiled at him.

"It is not that serious, boy. The hell are you so upset about? Because your mom is helping me? What did I ever do to make you hate me so much?"

"I ain't tryna hear that shit, Cee."

"Tryna hear what?"

He didn't reply.

"That's a damn shame. If that girl done made you hate me for some reason, that is so fucked up. When I left, we were crazy in love with each other. I don't understand what's changed."

"Ain't shit changed," Rell said.

He could not think of the reason why he was so upset with his mom for letting Ciara stay here. Ciara was certainly right about one thing: they had been madly in love when she left for Kansas. He missed her so much when she left that for many nights afterward he'd sat up in bed feeling a sickening sadness in his heart, unable to sleep, unable to think about anything but her. She had been his first love. He'd fucked a handful of girls before her, but none of them had taken control of his heart the way Ciara had.

He didn't want to think about it. The memories brought back feelings that he didn't want to feel. He loved Tamera now. Tamera was his world and she was the only woman he'd have those kinds of feelings for.

Ciara stepped in the room and swung the door shut.

Without looking back at her Rell said, "Don't do that."

"Don't do what?"

"Open the door back up."

"Dang, boy, do you think I'm about to kill you or something?"

Rell didn't say a word. He found a trash bag half full of clothes in his closet and started throwing his sneakers in it.

Ciara walked up behind him and put her hands on his shoulder.

He spun around and grabbed her by the arms and threw her to the bed.

Gazing up at him, she cracked a smile.

"You've got some serious aggression in you that needs to be taken care of," she said, as her hands rose slowly to cup her breasts. "Let me help you get rid of it."

King Rio

Chapter 19

Tamera was leery about driving toward Spaulding where Zo's gang hung out, so she led the way up 16th Street in the opposite direction, cautiously steering the clean Mercedes Benz ahead of her and Tirzah's gray Corvette. She hoped that Tirzah would be able to keep it together until they made it to the hotel. She was going to the Trump this time. With all the stress Rell and Jah's drama in the streets had her going through, she felt that she deserved a bit of luxury.

She scanned the street as she drove. She had her gun on her lap and she was afraid that this might just be the night that she would have to use it.

Her heart skipped a beat when a car full of guys rode up alongside her door and rolled down their windows to holler. She thought they were going to start shooting, and when they didn't, she sped off without giving them a word, bumping Nicki Minaj's "I Lied" through the Benz's speakers through the Bluetooth connection.

When she looked back and saw that Tirzah was keeping up, she eased back in her seat and turned up the music.

"You said you thought you was ready and I said 'let's see'
But I ain't mean that, I need some fucking proof
'Cause what happens if I fall in love, then you cut me loose?
You just a heartbreaker, won't let you break mine
'Cause I'll be smashing windows and cutting them brake lines..."

Tamera laughed at the part about cutting brake lines. She thought of Rell's ex-girlfriend and envisioned herself cutting his brake lines if she found out that he was fucking that bitch.

She knew that she would not hesitate to do it. She'd probably do a lot more than just cut a brake line if Rell cheated on her. She hated to admit it, but Rell had her dick-whipped. His sex was so good that she couldn't imagine him giving it to someone else. She would lose her mind if she learned that he'd ever cheated on her, because she knew that whoever he cheated with would never stop coming back for more.

"I gotta stop thinking so negatively," she said aloud to herself, lowering the music volume and shaking her head at herself. "I'll be done turned around and pulled up to that boy's momma's house on straight up bullshit."

Once out of the Lawndale neighborhood she felt a lot safer than she had while she was there. She and Tirzah stopped at a Taco Bell, and she told Tirz which hotel she'd decided on. Tirzah really didn't care about the hotel's location. All she wanted was a nice place to rest and settle her nerves.

Twenty minutes after their restaurant stop, they checked into two adjoining rooms at the Trump International Hotel & Tower. Tirzah got in bed with Tamera, and they held each other close.

"Call Jah for me and tell him what room we're in," Tirzah said in a near whisper.

Tamera ran her fingers through Tirzah's long braids and dialed Jah's phone number. He didn't answer until the second time she called.

"Yo, what's up, sis?"

"We're at the Trump. Rooms 711 and 712. How long before y'all make it here?"

"I don't know. Shit, I really don't even wanna come. I wanna stay out here and try to catch up with whoever offed my lil nigga Capone. I'm too sick about that shit. Everybody knows how much I loved that lil nigga. He was just as much as my bro as D-Lo was. This shit's crazy."

"I know what you mean," Tamera said, nodding her head as if he could see her agreeing with him. "I've had my own share of losses. It's a messed up feeling."

"Too fucked up, man." Jah's voice sounded like it was on the verge of cracking. "My lil nigga was only fifteen years old. A real nigga. Ain't never backed down from shit. Shit like this is why I stay strapped up day and night. I ain't going like that. I'm taking a mu'fucka with me if I'm going. It won't just be me. That's why I don't play games out here. Shit is way too real to be playing games with these niggas."

"Where's your brother? He said he was about to Facetime me."

"Aw, he'll be in here in a sec. He just got to doing something for Momma. I'll tell him to hit you. You said rooms 711 and 712, right?"

"Yeah. Tell him I said call me as soon as possible. We need to have a serious talk."

"I got'chu, sis." Jah paused. "Tell baby I said I love her. I promised her that we was gon' catch that fuck nigga Tremaine and I stood on my word. That should mean something. I know I'm young but I'm trying. That's all I can do is try."

"She recognizes your efforts." Tamera smiled down at Tirzah. "But I'll tell her, bro."

"A'ight. Thanks, sis."

Tamera stared at the screen of her smartphone for a long while after the call had ended, thinking of how much Jah must really love her big sister. She was just about to say it when Tirzah got up and went to the bathroom.

"Let me get in here and get myself together," Tirzah said. "I'm all crying and shit because I fucked up the nigga who raped me. We should be fucking celebrating."

"See, now, that's my motherfucking big sister!" Tamera beamed. "Fuck Tremaine, girl. He got exactly what the fuck he deserved."

"My lil baby came through."

"Jah is way more than a lil baby. He's a young man who's found his queen. You can't keep looking at him as a boy because of his age. He knows what he wants. He put that ring on your finger for a damn good reason, Tirz. For real. Don't take that shit for granted. Don't let that nigga Reese get to your head just because he got all that money. That shit don't mean a damn thing without love and loyalty. You can build with Jah and eventually you both will be millionaires. You feel me, big sis?"

"I do now." Tirzah walked into the bathroom doorway and looked out at Tamera, wiping her face with a wet washcloth. "Jah's a real nigga and I need to be his ride or die bitch until the end of time. I don't know what the fuck I was thinking."

"He just told me to tell you he loves you."

"I heard it through your phone. That's what made me get up and come in here to get myself together. I love his young ass just as much as he loves me."

"So," Tamera asked, feeling all giddy about the idea of true love, "are you still going to work at Redbone's tomorrow night or what?"

Tirzah shook her head no. "Fuck that. The only nigga I'ma be shaking this ass for is Jahlil Owens."

Tamera's heart warmed up in her chest. She smiled a genuinely happy smile and then got up and went to the suitcase she'd packed for herself and Rell before leaving the house. She dug through it and took out her most revealing piece of lingerie, along with a pair of five-inch Christian Louboutin heels that Rell had given her for Valentine's Day last night.

"We do got some real niggas in our lives," she said to Tirzah. "You can't name another bitch in the hood who got a ring on her finger. Niggas ain't even got the money to buy a ring, and if they do, they go out and blow it on Robin's and Trues. Ain't nobody getting wifed up like us. And look at how Reese was looking at us earlier. We got rich niggas looking at us like we're worth more than diamonds."

"Because we are," Tirzah said. She was at the sink mirror now, putting on some eyeliner. "We're worth more than gold. That's what Alicia Keys was talking about when she made that song "A Woman's Worth". Bitches these days aren't queens. They could never have been Nefertiti. Their nasty asses would have been lost in the crowd of slave-workers, building pyramids and shit."

Tamera could not repress the laugh that burst out of her. She shook her head as she joined Tirzah in the bathroom.

"Umm, I'm pretty sure that you and Jah have a bathroom in that room next door," she said, putting her hands on her hips and watching as Tirzah applied a layer of strawberry red lipstick to her puckered-up kissers.

Tirzah laughed and shook her head and continued to fix her face.

"I sent Tara a text letting her know what rooms we're in," Tamera said. "She said her and K are just gonna stay in tonight. They're gonna spend some time with their kids." She sat down on the toilet seat and again found herself gazing at her iPhone 6S. "I think we should just focus on what's important right now, Tirz. We need to be talking to Rell and Jah about a business. They have a little money now, and since we're about to be married to those crazy fuckers we need to be managing that little bit of money the way Dreka runs everything for Kevin Gates. We've gotta come up with some solid, realistic business plans to make sure that we never go back to where we started."

"Never another Janky drive, huh?" Tirzah laughed.

Janky was the nickname of the raggedy old Ford Taurus that Tamera's ex-boyfriend had gotten her.

"Definitely never," Tamera said, shaking her head at the memory of the piece of shit car. "From now on, we're going to take care of business like the boss bitches we were born to be."

"Can I get an amen?" Tirzah said excitedly.

"Amen!"

"Glory hallelujah!" Tirzah jumped around in circles, as if she'd suddenly been struck by the Holy Ghost.

Tamera's head fell back in laughter.

Within the next thirty minutes, she and Tirzah were all dolled up and ready to surprise their soon-to-be husbands with an unforgettable night.

Chapter 20

"Johnny, what you need to do is get that damn ring off Tamera's finger. I mean, if you really want to get some money. Diamond rings don't lose value. It's like having a savings account on your finger. I heard that ring is worth over a hundred thousand dollars alone. I'm telling you what's good for you. Your best move would be to get that ring and cash out with it. There's no way you can lose. I told Ciara to try and get it if she can, but that lil hoe just wants to fuck on Rell, thinking she might be able to get some money out of him. I told her like I'm telling you. Get the ring. The ring is where it's at. Catch Tamera at a stop light if you have to. Put a gun to that bitch's head and take that ring off her finger. It's as simple as that."

Shanita was whispering to Johnny B as she sat next to him in the passenger seat of his new car. He was rolling a blunt and nodding his head. He was listening closely, occasionally glancing out his window, past the members of the D Block gang of Vice Lords to the front windows of Maria's house.

He and Shanita were alone in the car. He liked Shanita a lot. Always had. All the guys liked her. She was an older woman with a killer body. Johnny B could not count on all his fingers and toes the amount of times he had jacked off thinking about fucking her, and he had a feeling that tonight was going to be the night when his dreams came true. She'd been all over him for most of the day, and he had a feeling that she knew who'd really killed Capone. She was one of those women who could read anybody.

"Keep your mouth shut about all this shit," Johnny B said. "Let me work my magic. Believe me, I know what I'm doing. I know exactly how to play this shit. I was bred for this kinda shit. But stop talking about it. You talk too much. Be done fucked up the whole lick running your mouth."

Shanita rolled her eyes at him, but she kept quiet.

Once Johnny B had the blunt rolled, he got back out of the car and rejoined the gang. Most of them were either drunk or on their way to being drunk. Johnny B was a little buzzed, but he was far from drunk, and he planned to keep it this way. He had to stay sober to think clearly. He still wasn't certain if he should take Zo up on the offer and whack Jah. He had a lot of love for Jah. Jah was a real killer like he was. As a matter of fact, Jah was an even bigger menace. If not for Jah's ruthless reputation, D Block would never have gained the respect and attention it now had in the streets.

There was a single chair on Maria's front porch. Steve, a twelve-year-old who had already dropped two bodies in the hood, was sitting in the chair doing something on his smartphone when Johnny B shoved him out of it.

"Fuck out my seat, lil nigga," Johnny B said.

Steve scowled at Johnny B and mumbled something under his breath as he shook the snow off his pants. A few of the guys turned their attention to the two shooters to see if there was about to be some action, but this was not the case. Steve said, "On my momma, boa...", and then walked off down the stairs. No one cracked any jokes on him, like they would have done had it been one of the other youngsters. Steve was a youngster, but he had far too much respect within the gang to be tried in such a way.

Johnny B called Steve back up onto the porch to hit the blunt when he lit it.

"I'm just fuckin' wit'chu, lil homie," Johnny B said, giving Steve a playful punch to the arm. "You know it's all love this way."

"On my momma, if it wasn't you, boa," Steve said, and filled his lungs with smoke.

Johnny B chuckled and turned his attention to the rest of the gang. They were all strapped with handguns, and several of them had assault rifles stashed away in bushes and in the trunks of cars. They were laughing and joking with each other but also keeping watch over the block. Every vehicle that passed was closely inspected. Every person who walked by was treated the same way.

There would be no catching the D Block gang lacking tonight.

Jah came outside a minute later. Johnny B watched him look at every face in the crowd.

"Lil Larry," Jah said, and Lil Larry came jogging up the stairs to join them.

Lil Larry was another young gangbanger, though he was a lot more cunning with his crimes. He was more likely to sneak someone, the way Johnny B had taken out Capone, than to simply open fire when there was a problem the way Jah usually did. He had long dreadlocks like Johnny B, separated into two ponytails over his ears.

"Bruh told me to lay this on you and Johnny B." Jah reached in his jeans pocket and took out two sandwich bags full of tan-colored blocks of a rocky substance that Johnny B instantly knew was heroin. "It's two zips of boy. One for you, one for you. He say he just want $75 for every gram. This shit pure bass, too, the same shit that nigga PJ used to pump over there on Millard, so you can step on it and bring it back and it'll still be that whip, you feel me? Y'all can keep coming back. We got the plug on this shit now. For a while, at least. We told him how hard it is out here, that we're just trying to eat. He say he'll put a whole brick to the side just for D Block."

"Aw, this shit'll be gone tomorrow, bruh," Lil Larry said, eyeing the dope as he handed Johnny B one of the bags.

Johnny B passed the blunt to Jah and tried calculating the profit he would make from selling the ounce of heroin. He figured that he would pocket at least $200 off every gram after paying youngsters who were around Steve's age to sell it for him, since they could not be charged as adults if they were ever to be caught with the product.

Looking at Jah out of the corner of his eye, Johnny B thought of the other $40,000 he would get when he finally got the chance to kill Jah. With the cash he already had, plus the money he would make off the dope and the $40,000 for Jah's murder, he would be able to afford a home. Maybe he would get into real estate and eventually own a bunch of houses like Rell and Jah.

"I wonder how a nigga was able to sneak Capone like that," Jah said thoughtfully as he passed the blunt to Steve. "That's the only part I'm confused about. Lil bruh never left out without that pole on him, and I can't see him just mobbin' with anybody. He was always with the squad."

"We had just ran a lil thot at y'all building on Douglas," Johnny B said, shaking his head with feigned shock. "He mobbed off down Douglas. Never saw lil bruh again."

"He had to have met up with somebody else," Jah said. "Somebody he trusted. That's the only thing that makes sense to me. I can't see that shit going down no other type of way."

"That's the same thing I said." Lil Larry sipped from his double-stacked Styrofoam cup of Lean and hit the Kush. "Lil bruh just knocked a nigga this morning. And he was into it with the Breeds, too. He knew better than to be out here lacking. That was some up close and personal shit. Whoever did that shit was with him."

"Had to be one of Zo's guys," Johnny B said.

Jah nodded. "Might've been. They just tried to get down on us before we got over here. Damn near hit us up. That's how we ended up in the car with Ms. Williams. They shot up the whip."

"The Benz?" Lil Larry asked.

Jah shook his head no, but didn't explain.

Then Rell walked out the door putting on his jacket and asked for a ride.

Johnny B said he would give them a ride, and once the blunt was finished they all got in his new gray Nissan Altima and headed for the Trump International Hotel & Tower.

King Rio

Chapter 21

Rell smelled like Ciara.

The scent of her perfume was all over him. He could smell it, Jah could smell it, and he knew that Tamera would smell it.

"Bruh, you better make sure Tamera ain't by her purse where that strap at when you walk in the room," Jah said, scooting away from Rell in the backseat. "Don't get that shit on me. I ain't tryna have Tirz all on my neck about it."

Rell waved off Jah's comment and said, "We might as well go on and get the weddings out the way, lil bruh. I mean in the next couple of weeks. I think it'll make our women a whole lot happier, and that's what they need right about now."

"Weddings?" Johnny B said from the driver's seat. "I know I'm invited."

"Hell yeah, bruh," Jah said. "You already know. I ain't inviting too many niggas, but I gotta have you and Lil Larry there."

"And me, right?" Shanita asked from the passenger seat. "I just wanna be there to get a look at that ring everybody's been sharing on Facebook." She looked back at Rell. "The ring you gave Tamera. That thing is a masterpiece."

Rell chuckled and rolled down his window. "Yeah, you can come. Just don't bring Cee Cee."

"Did y'all fuck?" Shanita asked.

Rell looked at her like she was crazy and then turned back to his window.

"Where we gon' do it?" Jah asked.

Rell shrugged. "Let them decide all that shit. All we gotta do is show up."

Jah laughed, but Rell was as serious as a heart attack. He didn't care where they got married. He just wanted to get it done. He felt that Tamera and Tirzah deserved it. The Lyon sisters had stuck it out with them through the roughest patch of their lives. Rell knew that he would more than likely never run into another woman as loyal and loving as Tamera. Jah could say the same for Tirzah. The two sisters were irreplaceable. Nothing could compare to being with them. Absolutely nothing.

Although Rell had promised to Facetime his lovely lady, he decided not to. For one, he didn't want Johnny B and Shanita all in his business. It was bad enough that they had managed to talk their way into his and Jah's weddings. He didn't need them sticking their noses in anything else.

He was also too caught up in his thoughts about Capone's murder.

He thought of the conversation between Jah and Capone he'd overheard while they had been waiting on Tremaine in the parking lot at Church's and tried to remember Capone's words, but then Johnny B turned up the volume on Jadakiss's Top 5 Dead or Alive album and Rell could not think so he just listened and stared out his window as they headed east down Roosevelt Road. He loved listening to "Kiss", but it was Lil Wayne's verse on the "Kill" track that got his attention.

"I'm in this bitch, kush in this Swisher
I'm with my niggas, y'all witnesses.
RIP to them fake niggas.
VIP for my skate niggas..."

Rell's attention shifted from the music to his iPhone when he received a text message from Tamera.

It was a video message, and Jah received one just seconds later.

Rell opened it, and his mouth fell open.

138

In the video, Tamera was naked with one knee on the sink, twerking and shaking her ass while Tirzah stood back and recorded the video.

He looked over at Jah's phone and saw that Tirzah was nude and dancing in that video with Tamera standing back and recording it.

"Aw, they are on one tonight," Jah said with a big smile on his face.

Rell was also smiling. He could not wait to make it to the hotel. He watched the video three more times before they finally made it to the Trump, and by then, he'd forgotten all about what he was thinking before Johnny B interrupted his thoughts with the music.

He gave Johnny B $50 for the ride and thanked him, then he and Jah hurried off into the Trump.

King Rio

Chapter 22

"I bet when they saw those videos they were like, "What the fuck?" I wouldn't be surprised if they stepped out of that elevator butt naked," Tamera said, looking at Tirzah as they stood in bathrobes just outside the doors to their hotel rooms, waiting on Rell and Jah to show up.

"Well, they're here," Tirzah said. "Jah said that they're on the way up now."

Tamera nodded her head, and her smile grew. She was practically naked underneath the bathrobe. Tirzah's Louboutin heels were almost identical to the ones she had on, and Tirzah had done an amazing job with their makeup.

Just then, the doors to an elevator down the hall slid open, and out of it stepped Rell and Jah.

Rell laughed. "Who the fuck are y'all supposed to be, Nicki Minaj and Beyoncé?" he said as he walked toward them.

"No," Tamera replied. "Just Tamera and Tirzah. That's it. The baddest bitches in Chicago. Nothing too major."

As soon as Rell made it to her, she mashed her lips against his and snatched him into the room, kicking the door shut as she disconnected the kiss and shoved him to the bed.

Which is when it hit her.

She frowned at him. "The fuck is that smell?"

He laughed and took off his jacket. "It ain't shit. Come here. I love you."

Tamera crossed her arms, cocked her head to the side, and squinted at him. She was trying to convince herself not to go ape-shit just yet. She'd give him a few seconds to explain. If that was not long enough, then she would grab the bottle of Ace of Spades champagne out of the ice bucket next to the bed and use it to attack him. She hoped that it wouldn't take the threat of violence to get the truth out of him but she was more than willing to take a try at it if all else failed.

"Please," she said, "don't make me get ratchet up in here. You smell like some kind of cheap-ass perfume. What the fuck is that smell? And where did it come from? I'm not gon' ask you again, Rell. I'm not in the mood to be fucking around with you, okay? Either you tell me what that smell is, or we have problems. Huge problems. What's it gonna be?"

Rell sighed and moved back on the bed. Kicking off his sneakers, he said, "You promise not to get mad?"

She went to the ice bucket and curled her fingers around the neck of the bottle. "Sure. I promise. I promise not to get mad. Just tell me."

"You better not hit me with that bottle."

"Talk," Tamera said.

"Put that bottle down. You gotta listen first. I don't want you swinging on me before you hear the whole story."

"Was it that ex bitch? Ciara? That's who it was, wasn't it?"

"Will you put the bottle down? Please?"

Tamera started crying without even meaning to. She dropped the bottle back in the bucket of ice, then turned and ran into the bathroom, slamming the door shut and locking it before Rell could reach it.

She put her back against the door and slid down to the floor. Her heart felt like it had been ripped out of her chest. Her hands trembled uncontrollably.

The doorknob shook as Rell tried to open the door.

"Baby, will you listen first? Damn."

"Get the fuck away from me, Rell. Just...get away. Go away. Go back to wherever the hell you just came from. I don't know what I was thinking trying to give you a good time. Fuck you!"

"Baby, will you please just listen to me? She was at my momma's house. That's where she's staying now. I didn't know it until I got there. As soon as I found out, I went to my room and started packing up all the stuff I had left over there. She came in the room grabbing all on me and shit. That's really all that happened. I even recorded the shit once she tried to give me the pussy, just in case your crazy ass went nuts on me about it. Here, look at it on my phone. On my life, I didn't do nothing wrong."

Tamera stood up quickly and opened the door. She took the phone out of Rell's hand and immediately closed the door in his face.

"If you're lying, the engagement's off, Rell. I mean that from the bottom of my heart. I'm not going through this shit again."

"Again?"

"You know what I mean."

"'Again' implies that I've done it before. That's bullshit because I know I've never cheated on you and never will, so that means you're comparing me to your exes again. I told you I'm not them. I'm a whole different nigga. I don't know how long it's gon' take you to realize that but you will eventually. I hope it's soon. I'm tired of that shit."

Tamera was in his photo and video gallery. She went to the most recently recorded video and pressed play.

It was a video of a brown-skinned girl lying back on the bed Rell had at Maria's house. The girl was licking her lips in a seductive manner and rubbing her breasts through the shirt she had on.

"Why are you taking a picture of me? Forget a picture. Get the real thing," Ciara said.

"I'm not taking a picture." It was Rell's voice. "I'm recording it to keep myself in the clear when my wife hears about this."

"Your wife?" Ciara sucked her teeth. "You ain't fucking married. Fuck that bitch. That dick was mine first. Tell that bitch you had to have some fun before you jumped the broom. She'll understand."

"Nah. I can't do it."

"Stop recording me, Rell."

"Stop seducing me."

"I'm not fucking playing. I came in here to give you what you've been missing, not to be on the next episode of *Cheaters*. Stop fucking playing with me and gimme that dick."

Tamera's nostrils were flaring as Ciara lifted her shirt and exposed her breasts to Rell. He laughed and turned the camera on himself.

"See, baby? See the shit I gotta go through looking this handsome? Got thots jumping in my bed like I ain't even engaged."

"Thot!" Ciara shouted.

Rell turned the camera back to Ciara and caught a brief glimpse of her embarrassed face as she reached out to grab him.

The camera moved wildly for a couple of seconds. When it refocused on Ciara, Rell's free hand was palming her face and pushing it away while she laughed as if he was only playing around with her.

"Unwrap your legs from my waist, please," he said calmly. "If I did to you what you're doing to me, you'd be screaming rape by now. You're looking real desperate, Cee. Stop this shit before I get serious on your ass."

Being called desperate set Ciara off. She ripped away from Rell and got up. He kept the camera on her as she stormed out of the bedroom. Then he closed and locked the door, set the smartphone on his old dresser with the camera facing him, and went back to packing his clothes.

Feeling relieved and more than a little embarrassed, Tamera opened the bathroom door with a hint of a smile on her face and gave the iPhone back to Rell.

He smiled like he'd just won the lottery. "See what I mean? Just plain crazy. Never wanna listen and just hear a nigga out. Crazy is your first response every time."

She flipped him two middle fingers as he thumbed away her tears.

"I love you, Tamera. I don't just be saying that shit to make you feel good. I say it because it's the truth. I know you might not believe it but, on my soul, it's the truth. I love you with all my heart, baby. Always and forever."

Tamera began crying again as she stared into Rell's gorgeous brown eyes, but this time the tears were out of love instead of anger.

She pushed the bathrobe off her shoulders and let it drop to the floor.

Rell's attention went straight to the revealing piece of red lingerie she had on. It was a "love-red" see-through lace halter babydoll, and it revealed all her private parts.

She lifted the hoodie Rell had on over his head and tossed it to the bed as she hopped up onto him and locked her legs around his waist. He felt all over her derrière as he moved to put her back against the wall next to the bathroom door.

"I hope you know it's no mercy for that crazy shit you just pulled," he said, slapping her on the ass.

She knew exactly what that meant. Her pussy quivered in anticipation of what was to come.

The putrid stench of Ciara's perfume became too much to handle. She pushed back from Rell and asked him to take a quick shower.

While he got in the shower, Tamera popped open the champagne and drank gulp after gulp after gulp. She did a few stretches and wished Tirzah wasn't busy with Jah so that they could talk about how she'd almost ruined her night a few moments prior.

She had an already-rolled blunt of OG Kush in her Michael Kors bag. She fired it up and took a deep pull, so deep that she coughed several times from it. She needed the Kush in her system for what she planned to do to Rell. She could suck his dick for hours when she was high, and that is exactly what she wanted to do. She wanted to prove to him not only that she was sorry for responding so heatedly to the scent of Ciara's perfume but also that she loved him more than she'd ever loved anyone else, and that she appreciated the person he was, the realness of his character.

She stared at the ring on her finger while she smoked and waited for him to come out of the bathroom.

Chapter 23

Rell soaped and rinsed numerous times to assure that Tamera would not push him away again. Then he got out of the shower and took care of his hygiene. His soap, deodorant, toothbrush, and other hygiene products were already in the bathroom. Tamera had brought them with her from the house.

He stood at the sink and smiled at his reflection in the mirror. He heard the soulful lyrics of a J. Cole song playing and remembered that Tamera had liked it when he'd played the rap artist's music during their last hotel visit. He smelled Kush smoke coming from outside the bathroom and gritted his teeth at the delicious scent of it. He took a deep breath, got down and did fifty pushups, and then walked out of the bathroom without a single piece of clothing on.

Tamera's mouth fell agape, as if she had never before seen him naked.

"Goodness gracious," she said, her eyes bulging as she gazed at his package.

He had done nothing to make his dick hard, but it was as hard as could be, poking straight out at his beautiful fiancée. She extinguished the blunt she was smoking, walked over to him, and squatted down in front of it. She stroked it and inspected it. She kissed its head and caressed his scrotum.

Looking down at her, he wondered how he'd managed to get such a stunningly attractive woman to be his fiancée. He was proud of himself for turning down Ciara. The situation with Ciara had made him realize just how much he loved and cherished Tamera Lyon. He hoped that she would have the same restraint if one of her exes ever tried her in a similar way.

Her tongue waggled on the head of his dick. She jacked it in her hands while gazing up at him. She spit on it and spread the saliva all over his thick love muscle.

Then she sucked the head in her mouth and held it there, sucking tightly, stroking his length in both hands. She'd told him before that he had the best of both worlds. His dick was both long and thick. His scrotum was big and heavy.

He stepped back to the wall and rested his back against it. He put a hand on Tamera's head and watched as she began to suck his dick in and out of her expertly sucking mouth. She looked so pretty doing it. So perfect. He could not think of a single woman who looked more beautiful than Tamera, not even Rihanna, and boy did he have a thing for Rihanna.

He pulled Tamera to her feet, flipped her upside down, and started kissing and inhaling the goodness of her delicious pussy. She smelled so good that his mouth watered as he thought of how good she would taste. He stuck a finger in her, sucked the juices off his finger, and then dug his tongue into her juicy nookie and got himself a nice long taste before he went to tonguing and sucking her clitoris.

She put his dick back in her mouth and really went at it this time, sucking him wildly and loudly.

There was a small desk with a softly-cushioned seat next to the bathroom door. Rell went to it and sat down, flipping Tamera over to her feet.

"Great," she said as she kneeled down between his legs. "I was starting to get dizzy. All that damn blood rushing to my head."

She laughed once.

Rell laughed with her.

Then she returned to sucking and massaging his heavy phallus.

She slapped it on her lips and sucked the head in her mouth and squeezed his balls all at the same time. She forced his dick to the back of her throat until she choked.

"Yeah," he said, grinning.

148

She took her mouth off him and said, "You'd better enjoy this, because it's the last time we're having sex until we get married."

"Shiiiiit. Nigga, we can go to the courthouse first thing in the morning and get that out the way ASAP."

"That's not gonna happen." She stroked his dick in her hands. "I want a beautiful wedding, Rell. I told you that already."

"Okay, baby. Whatever you want is what you'll get. You're right. Let's just hurry up and do it." Rell didn't want to argue with her at a time like this. He'd let her win for now.

At least until they got the sex out of the way.

She gripped his dick a lot tighter than usual as she sucked it. He leaned back and put his elbows on the short table, enjoying the warm feel of her mouth. He wanted to taste her again, but he would wait until she got her full taste of him first. With the way she was sucking him now, he wasn't sure if she was going to stop before he came or keep going.

If she kept sucking him after he came, there would be no more kisses.

Not tonight.

Thankfully, she did stop.

She rose to her feet with one hand clamped down on his dick and used it to pull him over to the easy chair by the window near the bed.

She sat down and lifted her legs, rolling her fingertips on her clitoris in a circular motion.

"Okay, it's my turn now." She bit down on her bottom lip. "Eat."

Rell ate.

He went to his haunches without a moment's hesitation and began sucking on her clitoris while at the same time digging two fingers inside her. She was wet and tight, perfectly ripe for his dick to slide right in, but first he wanted to suck an orgasm out of her.

She palmed the back of his head, mashing his face into her tasty treat. He held up her leg with one hand and jacked his dick with the other. The hand holding her leg moved to her breasts. He pinched at the nipples and filled his hand with her pillow-soft C cups.

Tamera tilted her head back and moaned. Her moan was followed by another set of moans and a thump on the door that connected their room to Tirzah's.

Rell had to smile.

Lil bro was over there putting in work.

"Jah, Jah, Jaaaah!" Tirzah's voice came through as clear as if she were lying down next to Rell and Tamera.

Tamera didn't seem to notice her sister's passionate screams. Either that or she was too lost in her own ecstatic moans to care about what was going on next door. She was holding her ankles to keep her legs pulled back as Rell's intense tongue lashing continued.

She hardly lasted five minutes before her body tensed up in orgasm. Rell's lips were sealed tight around her clitoris when it happened, and he didn't let up as her inner juices became outer juices. He grabbed ahold of her hips and kept sucking until she leapt over the back of the chair to escape from his heartless tongue.

Rell stood up, laughing and wiping his mouth. Tamera was also laughing as he walked around the easy chair to look down at her.

"Get up, jerk," he said, smiling.

"I'm, like, literally paralyzed from the waist down right now. You're gonna have to give me a minute."

"Come on." Rell lifted her up and draped her over his shoulder. He slapped and squeezed on her soft butt cheeks as he walked to the bed and set her down.

"Okay, maybe we can do this one more time before we get married," she said with a guilty giggle. "That shit felt fucking amazing."

"Mm-hmm. Just like this dick is about to feel."

"Oh, no. That's an entirely different feeling. That hurts. Your tongue doesn't hurt. Your tongue doesn't try to rip me in half. It's the dick that does that."

"Shut up. Ol' scary ass." He leaned over her and pressed his lips to the side of her neck as he placed the head of his perilous pole on her pussy and then slowly pushed it in.

Tamera sucked in an audible breath as he pushed himself in deeper. She put her hands on his shoulders and shut her eyes. Her face tightened, as did her vaginal muscles. Rell kissed her passionately, holding her legs on his shoulders and her face in his hands as he began to thrust.

With the music blaring from the television across the room from them, J. Cole became the soundtrack to their lovemaking.

"You know that feeling when you know you finna bone for the first time
I'm hoping that she won't notice it's my first time
I'm hoping that my shit is big enough to fuck with
And most of all I'm praying, 'God don't let me bust quick'…"

Although he knew that it hurt Tamera whenever he dug all the way in, Rell could not help himself. Her pussy felt like heaven, and he wanted in.

He shoved it all the way in and held it there. He was used to her fingers digging in his back when he did this, but instead, she clawed at his shoulders. Tears filled her eyes, and for a moment, she stopped breathing.

He kissed her succulent lips, then went back to his long, full strokes.

"I love you," he said, and he meant it.

Tamera tried to reply, but all she got out was "I...", followed by a moan that lasted until she was out of breath.

Rell turned her onto her side, lifted her leg up, and fucked her deeply, knowing that this position made her moan a lot more than any other position.

He liked how the Louboutin heels looked on her feet. There were gold spikes on the black fabric of the heels. When he'd purchased them yesterday for the exorbitant price of $1,400, he had thought that they were too expensive. But now he appreciated every dime spent. If a pair of $1,400 shoes made his lady happy, then he would buy her a pair whenever she wanted them if he could. Especially if times like this were guaranteed to follow.

He picked her up again and moved her to the side of the bed. He bent her over and held her hips in his strong brown hands and fucked her until she screamed.

"Mm. Best pussy on earth," he said, leaning forward to plant a kiss on the middle of her back.

He slapped his hand across her ass and went even faster as he felt the tingle in his scrotum of an imminent eruption. Tamera threw it back as she looked over her shoulder at him, obviously sensing that he was about to ejaculate.

He dug all the way in again and listened to her moans as his dick twitched and dumped its load of cum inside her.

She tried to slip down to the floor when he finally pulled out of her, but he picked her up and lay her on the bed before stretching out beside her and letting out a heavy, relaxing breath.

"Damn. Fuck," he said.

"I concur," Tamera said.

It took Rell a few minutes to gather the energy to talk. He said, "I love you so much, baby. Thanks for being you. You're better than I ever imagined my wife would be. I can't wait to give you my last name."

"And I can't wait to take it, Rell."

"Just set a date. As soon as possible. I'm ready whenever you are. Oh, and by the way, we gotta invite Johnny B and Shanita. I promised them that they could come."

Tamera shrugged. "Hey, it's your wedding, too. If you want them to come, that's fine with me."

King Rio

Chapter 24

The Lyon sisters and Owens brothers spent the following week at the Trump, occasionally venturing out to the store and to look at homes. Rell and Tamera finally decided on a quarter-million-dollar home that was not in the Lawndale neighborhood and moved in days later. It was a four-bedroom home far north of Lawndale. 5951 West Grace Street.

Rell paid cash for it.

He and Jah also paid cash for their pair of white S550 Mercedes Benzes and the matching E350 Benzes they got for Tamera and Tirzah.

Jah and Tirzah found a house just a couple of blocks away from the Grace Street home for about the same price.

They set their wedding dates for March 2nd, the day after Jah's eighteenth birthday.

At 6:54 P.M. on the evening of Jah's birthday, Rell and Jah were dressed to impress in all-white Balmain shirts and jeans, twin pairs of snow white Louboutin sneakers, and brand-new white leather Pelle Pelle jackets to coincide with the clean white Benz they would be pulling up to the club in for their bachelor party.

"This gon' be our last night being single men," Jah said as he and Rell stood at the dresser mirror in Rell's bedroom, thumbing through the bankroll he'd just gotten from Lil Larry for four more ounces of heroin.

Tirzah sucked her teeth and scowled at Jah. She was sitting on the foot of the bed, and Tamera was still in the bathroom getting dressed.

"You know what I meant, baby," Jah said.

"Mm-hmm. Look at you," Rell said with a laugh. "About to get beat up on your birthday."

"Man, I wish a nigga would touch me. I'm a grown-ass man now. Ain't no more games."

Rell had to laugh again. Ever since Jah woke up this morning he'd been claiming to be a grown man now, as if turning eighteen was the most adult thing that could have happened to him.

Tirzah shook her head and sighed. "It's cool. We got five male strippers waiting to show out for us. Y'all go and have fun, 'cause me, Tamera, and Tara are about to have a ball, baby. You can believe that. With your grown ass."

Jah's expression turned serious. "A'ight. Get them niggas fucked up."

"Whatever, boy."

"On my momma I'm dead mu'fuckin' serious. You already know how I'm rockin'. Get a nigga shit pushed back tryna play them flirting games."

Tirzah rolled her eyes and went off to join Tamera in the bathroom.

"We should pop up on them and see what the fuck they got going on tonight," Jah suggested, still counting the money. "I don't trust that male stripper shit."

"Nigga, we got strippers too," Rell reasoned as he brushed his hair and studied himself in the mirror. "Don't start tripping. Let them do them. We'll have fun, they'll have fun, and tomorrow we'll be married men. That's all there is to it."

"I'ma be a locked up man if she let some stripper nigga put his dick all in her face."

Rell could not help but to laugh at his younger brother's jealousy. He finished brushing his hair and put the hairbrush in his back pocket.

"I'm nervous as fuck about tomorrow," Jah muttered. "You think I'm too young to get married? I mean, damn, I did just turn eighteen today. Maybe I'm going too fast."

"You can't go wrong with a bad chick like Tirzah, bruh. She's all you need. Ain't no reason to be nervous. You're good. Everything's gon' be straight. Don't even worry about it. Just show up and say those vows and be faithful to her until the end of time. Everything else will work itself out."

"You talk to Johnny B? I ain't heard from bruh since early this morning."

Rell shook his head. "Nope. Ain't heard from him."

"He still coming to the wedding?"

"I guess so. He said he was coming. I know he better bring that money. He owe us forty-two hundred."

"That's probably why his ass ain't called nobody," Jah said.

Just then, Tirzah came back in the room and told Rell that Tamera wanted him in the bathroom.

He collected his half of the $8,400 that Lil Larry had just paid them for another four ounces of heroin and pocketed it as he headed into the bathroom with Tamera.

She was standing in front of the six-foot mirror that hung on the wall next to the toilet, checking herself out from the side. She had on a skin-tight red dress that went along perfectly with her black-and-red Giuseppe Zanotti heels. Her ass looked so good in the dress that it made Rell mad.

Tamera had stuck to her word.

She was holding out on the sex until after their wedding.

"How do I look?" she said, so caught up in her own reflection that she didn't bother to look at his. If she had looked at him she would have seen that he was not happy to see her looking so incredibly beautiful.

"You look great." Rell's voice was dripping with sarcasm.

"Well, I'm glad you think so. I really wasn't so sure about these heels. I'm thinking about switching to those Louboutins you bought me for Valentine's Day. I only wore them that one time at the hotel. I think they'll look much better with this dress than these Giuseppes."

"This no sex shit ain't gon' cut it, baby. On God. I can't go for it tonight. You gon' have to suck on this mu'fucka or something. I don't care what you do to it, but you better make this mu'fucka bust."

Finally, Tamera's eyes moved to his reflection, and she smiled her perfect smile. Her hands went to her hips.

"You are oh so serious, aren't you?" she said.

"Don't smile at me, like it's funny. It ain't funny. It's the furthest thing from funny. This shit is torture. You're trying to kill me before we get married."

"No, no, no," she said, turning and walking to him, "I'm going to kill you on our honeymoon, if you get my drift." She put her arms on his shoulders and interlaced her fingers on the nape of his neck. "Can you believe that we're actually getting married tomorrow? Oh, my God, I'm so nervous. I hope everything goes as planned. Hope my mom doesn't act an ass. She's known to be a little messy. Me and Tirz call her the queen of petty. And I hope your mom acts right, too, because I remember how she talked to me when I first met her. Her ratchet ass."

"Don't call my momma ratchet, nigga."

"I meant it in a good way."

"Yeah, and I'ma mean it in a good way when I push you down the stairs."

Tamera laughed and pressed her face into the crook of his neck. He moved his hands down her back and grabbed two big handfuls of derrière. She smelled so good. Much better than the funky perfume that had almost cost him his life at the Trump hotel two weeks ago. Her body was so tight that he could not understand why she had been working out lately. He stared wantonly at the reflection of her ass in the mirror behind her, wishing that his face could be nestled between her pillowy cheeks.

"Thank you so much, Sincere. For everything. I really mean it. I know that I'm not the most sane woman in the world, but I try my best to be the perfect woman for you. You make me so happy. I honestly never thought I'd be this happy. You don't understand how grateful I am to have you in my life. You could have easily just treated me like a one-night stand and went on with your life. I could've done the same thing, but I saw the good in you. I saw it in your eyes. I felt it when you first touched me. You're the most honest, loving man I've ever met in my life, and I just want you to know that I don't and never will take you for granted. I'll always love and appreciate you for the good man you are."

"Really?" Rell's eyes were still stuck on her ass. "Prove it to me."

"Nuh uh." Tamera backed up, grinning and shaking her head no. "You ain't slick, nigga. Your ass is going to wait. I'll do all the proving you want me to do on our honeymoon."

She went back to the mirror, swinging her hips a lot harder than usual.

Rell watched with clenched teeth as she adjusted the snug dress and went back to scrutinizing herself in the mirror.

"I don't know how comfortable I am with Shanita coming to our wedding," she said. "I don't trust that bitch after her niece tried you like that. For all I know, she could've told that lil thot to do that trifling shit. I feel like the bitch really came for me."

"Ain't nobody came for you. Crazy ass." Rell sat down on the edge of the bathtub and pulled out his iPhone. "Only reason she wanna come is because of Johnny B. If it wasn't for him coming, she would've never tried to come."

"I should be ultra petty and have her turned around at the door."

"Why is everything 'petty' with you?"

"Because I'm my momma's child."

"Man, fuck that shit. Let that woman come and enjoy herself. You know Johnny B just moved in with her and everything. She's in love with bro. Let the cougar have fun with her young nigga."

"I don't see why you call that nigga your bro. Jah is your bro. I keep telling you not to be trusting these niggas in the streets. The streets don't love nobody. Never have, never will. Motherfuckers are snakes. Wolves in sheep's clothing. Ever heard that saying before?"

Rell nodded his head.

"Well," Tamera sailed on, "you better recognize game. You never know what's going on in somebody else's head. Especially when they ain't family. Niggas will cut some steak for you and then stab you in the back with the same damn knife. And this is Chicago. Chiraq. Niggas will stab you in the face with the knife, forget your back. You know I ain't lying."

"Will you shut that shit up so I can call Johnny B about this money?" Rell said, giving her attitude not because of what she was saying but because he wanted some pussy and she wasn't budging.

He dialed Johnny B's phone number, turned on the speakerphone, and struggled to keep his eyes off Tamera's assets while it rang.

"I'm on the way over there now with that bread," Johnny B said as soon as he answered. "Need four more zips, too. Man, this shit selling like hot cakes. D Block got the whole hood sewed up. I'm thinking about getting a truck next week. Fuck it. Might as well flex on niggas. Do it for D-Lo and Capone."

"Capone World," Rell said, because everyone on D Block was now repping "Capone World" in honor of Capone's legacy.

"All day, joe," Johnny B said. "So, uhh, what's up with the bachelor party? We still on? I'm ready to see some big booty bad bitches bustin' it open to some 2 Chainz or somethin'. Let's get this shit crackin', bruh. On Capone. I got a stack to throw at the hoes. Make it rain a lil bit, you feel me." Johnny B laughed.

Tamera twisted her face at the laugh and silently mouthed, "Fake-ass nigga."

"My wife said hi," Rell said.

"Aw, shit, tell sis I said what's crackiiiiiin'! Tell her I said we gon' T up at the wedding. I'm bringing my own drinks."

Tamera rolled her eyes and didn't reply.

"Aw, speaking of the party," Johnny B said, "Shanita wanna know if she's invited to the bachelorette party."

Rell looked over at Tamera and smiled. She shook her head no, cutting a hand across her throat and mouthing, "No! No! No! No!"

"She said yeah," Rell said. "Tell her to come on over before they leave. Or just meet up with her and Tirzah at the Manhattan strip club on Ashland. It's a bunch of naked white boys, so make sure you don't step in there with her."

Rell ducked and fell over in the bathtub as a toothbrush came flying at his head. He laughed out loud. Johnny B took it as him laughing at the strip club.

"You know I ain't walking in on no shit like that, fam. Never me. We're almost there, bruh. About twenty minutes. Open the door."

"A'ight. Capone World," Rell said, and ended the call.

"I should find something to break over your goddamn head, Rell. I am so fucking serious. Ugh, I can't stand you."

"Gimme a kiss," Rell said, poking his lips out.

"Kiss my ass."

"I'll kiss it. Bring it over here. I'll do more than kiss it."

"I ain't bringing you a damn thing. And I hope you know you just lost your chance for some pussy tomorrow night. We're gonna be laid up doing nothing for our honeymoon. Sorry to tell you."

Rell's brows came together as he stood up. He reached out and grabbed Tamera's elbow. Pulling her to him, he swung his other hand onto her ass and gave it a harsh squeeze.

"Ouch! You fucker!" she said. "Let go of my arm. And my ass. Please. I'd very much appreciate it."

"Nah, you got me fucked up on this holding back shit. I ain't on that."

Tamera crossed her arms over her chest and stared into his eyes. Rell didn't back down; he kept a serious face and did not loosen his grip on her ass and elbow.

"You must really wanna get fucked up today," she said. "That's all I'm seeing right now. Get your hands off—"

Rell mashed his lips against hers and kissed her like a man who'd just served two decades in prison and was just now laying his eyes on the woman he loved. His dick got hard almost instantly; he thrust his hips forward so that Tamera could feel it, just to let her know what he was feeling. He was surprised when she began kissing him back. Her hands roamed up and down his broad back.

"I'm sorry," she said.

"Damn right you're sorry," Rell said.

"I love you."

"I love you...too." He slipped his fingers under her dress and raised it up over her thick butt cheeks. He moved one hand around to her stomach and then pushed it down into her panties and stuck his middle finger inside her.

She shoved down his hand and snatched open the bathroom door.

"Later," Tamera said. "I promise."

Rell could only watch her walk away.

She left him standing there in the bathroom with the front of his jeans poking out from his waist.

King Rio

Chapter 25

"I want that shit done tonight. No excuses. At least get Jah out the way. Either that or just gimme back my ten racks. I don't want that nigga to live to see his wedding tomorrow. If my lil bruh can't get married, then that nigga Jah can't get married. Period."

Zo's teeth made a snapping sound as they collided with each other. He was pacing a tight circle in the living room of Zaniyah's house, smoking a Newport cigarette that was just an inch away from the green line at the filter. His .40-caliber pistol was gripped tight in his left hand. Fourteen of his closest friends were standing around the room smoking blunts and sipping iced Lean. Two of them had assault rifles in hand, even though there were two police cars parked up the street at the corner of 16th and Spaulding.

A couple of the neighborhood girls were sitting on the sofas with Zaniyah and Lisa. They were doing all kinds of drugs, from Kush to pills and coke. None of them looked as visually appealing as they appeared on their social media pages. There were no fancy heels or Michael Kors bags or expensive weaves. No, they were in full trap mode today: ponytails, Air Force Ones, and jeans.

Their unkempt appearances were understandable. It was not like they had any parties to attend. With Zo's gang being at war with not only Jah's gang but also two other sets, the block was on fire. The hood was so hot that mostly everyone was staying inside. There was no need to dress like they were going out to the club. They were stuck in the house with a bunch of trap niggas.

"I'm on my way to handle this shit right now, Zo. Chill the fuck out. Told you I got you," Johnny B said.

Zo hung up on Johnny B and threw the smartphone onto Zaniyah's lap. She jumped; she was so high off Xanax pills that he caught her off guard, even though she'd been staring right at him. She let out a light laugh and went back to staring emptily at him.

He went to the living room window and looked out the blinds just as one of the cop cars went driving off down Spaulding. His big sister, Odella, was on her porch across the street, arms crossed, looking up and down the street, being nosy as usual. Patricia, their mother (who had not left Odella's house ever since she'd realized that Zo had some money) was standing right next to Della with a cigarette in her mouth.

"This nigga Jah think it's a game with me," Zo said, more to himself than anything. "He really thinks I'm playing with him. Nigga took my brother's life. Somebody gotta die about that. Real fucking soon. If Johnny B don't get to that nigga first I'm gon' have to do it myself."

"Baby, just..." Zaniyah said, but she didn't finish her sentence. She simply gazed at him as if he should understand the rest of her thought without hearing it.

"You need to get off that shit and stay off it," Zo said, turning back to the window.

He waited for the second CPD squad car to leave before he went outside and got in his Cadillac CTS. Zaniyah got in the passenger seat, and Zo sped off before the cops had a chance to pop back up, ignoring his sister and mother as they waved for him from across the street. Three Chevys full of his guys followed behind him.

"I would say drive over there to Rell and Jah's old house on Trumbull," Zaniyah said, "but some other niggas just moved in there today. I think Rell and Jah own that house, too. Think they're renting it. They got, like, ten houses, I think. At least ten. Probably more. Plus, they own that apartment building on Douglas. They got some real money, man. Shit is crazy. They came up just like you did. In no time. All because of their daddy dying. Wish I owned a damn house or a damn apartment building."

Zo looked over at Zaniyah and regarded her with a disgusted expression. He couldn't believe that he had wanted her so badly back when he was broke. He saw now that she was just like the rest of the neighborhood girls. All she wanted to do was get high and drunk and fuck. This morning she'd left to go to the store with one of his workers and when she returned, her breath had reeked of semen. When he asked her what the smell was, she blamed it on a bag of chips and immediately rushed off to the bathroom to freshen up.

"I know what that smell was in your mouth this morning," he said, the right side of his upper lip raised in disgust. "I wasn't born yesterday."

Her eyes widened a little, and she hesitated before replying.

"Sour cream and onion potato chips—"

"Yeah, a'ight."

"What? What do you think it—"

"Bitch, lie again and see if I don't cut you off right here and now. You know I don't love no hoes. It ain't like the shit gon' break my heart. What you ain't gon' do is sit here in my face and lie to me like I'm some lame-ass nigga. Keep it a hun'ed or get out my car and stay the fuck away from me. Period."

Zaniyah sighed and shook her head. She stared straight ahead as he drove up 16th Street. He waited on her to reply, but she remained silent.

"I'll take that as a confession," he said.

"Whatever, Zo."

"The fuck you mean whatever? You sucked his dick and lied to me about it. Be real about the situation."

Zaniyah rolled her eyes and sucked her teeth, just as Zo was pulling up to his cousin Joseph's house on 16th Street and Drake Avenue.

Her attitude set Zo off, though he didn't show it right away. He got out of the Cadillac and looked around the dark street as his guys climbed out of their cars. He was imagining himself shooting Jah in the face as the wild young Owens brother ran up on him from out of nowhere.

Zaniyah walked up to Zo and muttered, "I'm sorry. I should have—"

The slap sent her slamming into his driver door. He slapped her so hard that everybody stopped and looked at her.

A few of the guys shouted, "Damn!"

Zo grabbed a fistful of her hair as she tried to get up and with his right hand (he was right-handed) he punched her in the mouth. He was surprised when a couple of teeth divorced her gumline and flew onto the hood of his Cadillac. He punched her in the eye and the jaw. She screamed for help, but no one came to her aid. She covered her face as best as she could, but his fist kept pounding on her until he managed to knock her out cold.

He threw her to the ground, pulled the gun from his hip, and aimed it at her head.

"Don't do it, Zo!" Lisa shouted.

Apparently, watching her friend get the dog shit kicked out of her was okay, but observing the shooting of her friend would be too much.

Zo needed a moment to think.

He pointed the pistol at the dark sky and let off a thunderous shot before he started walking up the block toward 16th

Street, his head lowered, his eyes on the snowy, cracked sidewalk.

He squeezed off four more shots into the sky and growled.

Today was Jah's birthday, and Jah was somewhere in the city celebrating, enjoying life, preparing to get married tomorrow, which only added to Zo's frustrations. He felt that Jah should never have made it to see this day. Johnny B was supposed to have killed Jah by now. If Johnny B didn't get it done tonight, Zo planned to send his guys at Johnny B first thing tomorrow morning. He was tired of waiting.

Just as Zo made it to the corner of 16th Street and Drake Avenue, a police car pulled up right in front of him. It was one of the squad cars that had been parked on Spaulding moments prior.

Two policemen got out of the car with their guns drawn and aimed at Zo.

"Freeze! Chicago police! Drop the weapon now! Drop the weapon!"

Zo tossed the gun in one direction and took off running in the other. He made it to the other side of the street, and then the gunfire started.

What felt like a dozen bowling balls slamming into his back knocked him to the ground. Puffs of dust and dirt rose from the ground in front of his face as he lay flat on the street, numb and afraid and unable to move. He realized that the puffs were bullets hitting the ground, missing his head by mere inches.

He could not believe that he was still alive when the gunfire stopped. He couldn't feel anything, but he could see. He could see the growing pool of blood spilling out from under him. He could hear the screams of his friends as they cursed the police, and the screams of the policemen urging them to stay back.

Suddenly, he experienced an overwhelming sense of peace, and he heard his brother Roddy say, "It's okay, big bro. We're good now. We're good now. Come with me."

Then he died.

Chapter 26

Tirzah Lyon was moaning way too loud and as badly as she wanted to quiet down, she knew that it would be close to impossible with the way Jah was nailing her from behind.

She had tried to hold off on having sex with him until after the wedding, the same way Tamera was doing with Rell, but Jah had just thrown her face-down onto the bed in Rell and Tamera's guest bedroom, raised her flawless white Emilio Pucci dress, slid her white-lace panties to the side, and roughly shoved his dick inside her. Now, biting down on the knuckle of her middle finger, she was gazing vacantly at the pillows at the head of the bed while Jah fucked her. He had a pretty good sex game for an eighteen-year-old. Jah was packing eleven inches of goodness, which probably was Tirzah's reason for not fighting him about this unfortunate incident.

"Tirz!" Tamera shouted from outside the bedroom door. "Y'all in there fucking? Bitch, I could've sworn we agreed to wait until our honeymoons! Come on, we're supposed to be leaving out the door right now."

"Get on with that hater talk," Jah said. "We ain't on that."

"He's raping me," Tirzah said with a giggle as she arched her back and threw her ass at him.

"Y'all ain't shit." Tamera left the door, shouting for Rell.

Just then, Jah pulled his long love muscle out of Tirzah and started rapidly stroking it.

Not wanting to end up going to the bachelorette party with cum on her dress, Tirzah turned around to face Jah and crammed his dick to the back of her throat just as it started gushing out its salty protein.

Eyes watering, she looked up at him as he dropped his head back and groaned, thrusting into her mouth with his hands on his waist. His semen felt like thick gravy going down her throat, and there was so much of it that she gagged, but she kept him in her throat until he looked down at her and stepped back.

His dick popped out of her mouth. She studied its glistening length for a second, then dipped forward and tongued up the last drop of semen as it oozed out of him.

"Damn, I love yo' lil nasty ass," he said, wearing a smile that was just as bright as the diamonds in his Jesus piece. "You gotta do that on our honeymoon."

Tirzah rolled her eyes, picked up her Empire edition MCM bag, and stood up as Jah pulled up his boxer-briefs and jeans. She stepped around him and went to the door.

"Be good at that bachelor party," she said as she opened the door.

"You just make sure you don't have no stripper dicks all up in your face. Don't worry about me. Me and big bruh gon' be straight. We ain't tryna fuck none of them busted-ass bitches. We gon' turn up and leave. I'm tryna hurry up and get back home to you."

"I don't know what for. Ain't no more sex until after we're married tomorrow."

"Yeah, a'ight. That's my pussy you got. I can get that mu'fucka whenever I want it."

"You're a rapist," Tirzah said as she swung open the door and headed out into the hallway.

Jah followed her out of the bedroom, and they went to the living room where they found Rell and Tamera standing at the front door waiting on them with angry expressions on their faces.

"Bitch, I should kick you in your goddamn throat," Tamera said.

Both Jah and Tirzah busted out laughing, and even Rell could not hold back a laugh.

"Ain't shit funny," Tamera said. "Come on, hoe. Tara just pulled up. We gotta go."

Tirzah turned to Jah and blew him a kiss before she put on her coat (a white leather Prada coat that she'd talked Jah into buying her earlier today) and went walking out the door behind Tamera, thinking that maybe she'd stop somewhere for a small bottle of mouthwash before they made it to the strip club. She didn't need the handsome hunks of men shying away from her on the night before her wedding.

Tara's husband, K, passed them on the stairs. Tara was sitting behind the wheel of hers and K's white Trailblazer, talking on her smartphone. She waved and pushed open her door when she saw them.

"We'll take my car," Tamera said. "I know you ain't got no kinda gas in yours."

Tirzah rolled her eyes, smirking at Tamera because she was right.

They got in Tamera's sparkling white Benz, and Tara got in the backseat seconds later.

"Where are the boys going?" Tirzah asked.

"Redbone's," Tara said. "They're waiting on Johnny B to get here so they can all leave together."

"I don't know why they hang with that boy Johnny B." Tamera started the engine and waited for the car to warm up. "He seems really shady to me. And y'all know how that jealousy goes. Niggas see another nigga winning and automatically start hating and plotting. They feel like people owe them something. I find it hard to believe that Johnny B is content with riding around in that Altima when Rell and Jah are pushing S550s and buying houses. Even though Johnny B's seeing a little money on D Block now, in my opinion, he still ain't to be trusted. Or maybe it's just me thinking like that. Maybe I'm being too cautious."

"Girl," Tara said, "it ain't no such thing as being too cautious. I think it's fishy anyway that Johnny B was the last nigga with Capone before he got found dead. I can't pick who my cousins hang with, but trust and believe that you ain't the only one who don't like seeing Johnny B around Jah and Rell. I wish they would leave his snake ass in the hood where they met him."

"It's all good," Tirzah said, nodding her head in agreement with the girls. "I'ma put an end to that shit real quick, watch. Not about to have my husband around no nigga like Johnny B."

"And we ain't about to be hanging with Shanita, either," Tamera added.

Tara said, "What's wrong with Shanita? That's my bitch. She's cool people, for real for real. But I feel you. If she's with Johnny B, then keep her ass out the circle, too. No new friends."

"We'll kick it with her tonight," Tamera said. "Depending on how she acts, she might stay in the squad, but I don't know just yet. We gotta see if the bitch acts right first before we make any decisions."

"I'm with you when you're right," Tirzah said as she watched Rell, Jah, and K walk out onto the porch.

Tamera pulled off from the curb. She and the girls waved goodbye to their men as she drove away.

"What about Shanita?" Tirzah asked, digging in her purse for her sack of Kush.

"She'll have Johnny B's car," Tamera said. "Just hush and roll up. I wanna be on the moon by the time we make it to this club."

"Magic Mike action!" Tara shouted, throwing her hands in the air.

"More like Chocolate City," Tamera said. "I hope so, at least."

Chapter 27

Rell had big plans for the night.

He could not wait to get to Redbone's and lay his eyes on Bubbles, the baddest stripper he'd ever seen. She was reddish-brown in complexion and just as thick from the waist down as Tirzah. In fact, Tirzah was the only girl he knew who could match the perfect thickness that Bubbles possessed, and since his little brother had Tirzah on lock, Rell's only chance at seeing anything close to Tirzah twerking was seeing Bubbles do it.

He had $2,000 in singles to throw at the strippers. He had called in beforehand to see if Bubbles was working. She was. The guy who'd answered the phone told him that Bubbles and a number of other dancers would be performing onstage at the club tonight, and Rell could not wait to see her.

Rell and the guys stood on the front porch for almost ten minutes before they finally gave up on waiting outside for Johnny B.

"He ain't even answering his phone now," Jah said. "I done called four times. Keep getting the voicemail."

"Fuck it, let's sit in the car and blow one," Rell said. "If he ain't here by the time the blunt gone, we'll just leave his ass."

Jah and K nodded their heads in agreement.

The trio started off down the stairs. Rell hit the button on his electronic key that unlocked the doors to his Mercedes Benz S550 as they approached it. He got in the driver's seat and immediately began scrolling through his smartphone to find the perfect anthem to smoke to. He decided on a song an older cousin of his had gotten him hooked on a while back: Styles P's "Good Times".

"This that shit right here," K said from the backseat as he split open a White Owl cigar. "Man, I can't wait to get to that club, boa. I gotta see Bubbles make that mu'fucka clap. Wifey might get mad at a nigga tonight."

"They gon' be on the same shit we on." Jah passed a sandwich bag full of Kush to K. "I can't lie; I wanna see Bubbles my damn self. Y'all know she used to fuck with that rap nigga Bulletface? Know she gotta have some fire pussy for a billionaire rap star to be fucking with her like that. Especially with Bulletface being married to Alexus Costilla. I can't imagine being married to one of the baddest bitches in the world, who also happens to be the richest bitch in the world, and cheating on her with a stripper. But if it's any stripper that'll make a nigga do it, it's most definitely Bubbles."

"Y'all know lil homie who owns Redbone's is my nephew, right?" K said. "That's my sister's son. His daddy left all that shit to him."

"You need to tell that lil nigga to give you about ten million," Rell joked.

"Nah, that's his money. He don't owe me nothing. Long's he look out for his momma, I'm happy. He just bought her a mansion somewhere out in Bellwood. And he gave me twenty thousand. I ain't asking for no more than that."

"Yeah, I feel you," Rell said. "My people been on me about the lil money I got from my pops. I don't understand that shit. I feel like if I owed anybody, I'd pay 'em, and when I come around, bottles on me, you feel me? But for me to give away my wealth, to some niggas who ain't gave me shit? What kinda sense that make? Don't get me wrong, if I fuck around and come up on $10 million or some big money like that, yeah, I'm giving money to everybody, but I don't feel like I got enough to do that shit right now. Right now I'm still in grind mode. I'm tryna have me some kids sometime soon and be prepared to take care of them until they're grown. That's what's important to me."

"Same here," K said.

Rell became thoughtful. He looked from K to Jah and finally said, "It's fucked up how Capone got hit up like that. The more I think about that shit, the more I think it's something Johnny B ain't told us. I'ma ask him about that shit tonight. Jah, remember when you talked to Capone that day? Didn't he say something about him and Johnny B buying a new car?"

Jah nodded. "Yup. Well, he didn't say Johnny B, but he did say he had just bought a car with somebody. Said it was an Altima, too. I asked Johnny B about the car when he got it, though. He said he bought it."

"Cold-blooded," K said thoughtfully. "I wouldn't be surprised if homie was involved with that shit. You never know with niggas in these streets nowadays. Can't trust nobody. I don't think Johnny would whack the lil homie over a car, though. If he did do it, I'm guessing it had to be over something more serious."

"Man," Jah said, "will you niggas stop with all this mu'fuckin' talkin' and fire up? I'm tryna smoke."

"You look like you tryna smoke," K said. "Dave Chappelle head ass. 'I wanna talk to Samson' lookin'-ass boa. *Half Baked* face-ass boa."

They all laughed. Rell turned up the music and adjusted his seat.

"I get a rush off the blood on the walls, you understand?
Like the M-5 pedal, when it's touchin' the floor
I get high 'cause fuck it, what's better to do?
And I'ma never give a fuck 'cause I'm better than you..."

The Styles P song went along perfectly with the clouded inside of Rell's Mercedes Benz. He and the guys coughed incessantly. The Kush was some of the best weed they'd had in a while. Tamera had gotten it from a white guy she used to work with at Dunkin Donuts, a guy who Jah had robbed for a couple of pounds shortly after they met.

Wondering where Johnny B was and why Johnny's phone was suddenly turned off, Rell checked his rearview mirror and saw that Tamera's Benz was pulling back up. She had apparently circled the block for some reason. He was turning back to look at Jah and tell him that the girls were back when it happened.

A masked man holding a handgun with a long clip hanging out from under it came running out from beside the house, taking aim at the passenger door of the Benz.

Neither Rell nor Jah had their guns out, which was rare for them.

K said, "Oh, shit!"

Rell winced as the gunfire started.

Chapter 28

The masked gunman didn't get a single shot off.

Tirzah had told Tamera to go back to the house because she had left her bag of Kush with Jah and they didn't have any weed to smoke before hitting the club.

She had one of the Glock pistols she'd purchased for her and Jah a month ago in her purse, already cocked and ready to fire, when Tamera returned to the house on Grace Street.

As soon as Tirzah saw the man running out from beside the house, she snatched the gun out of her purse and emerged from the passenger door with her gun raised.

She took aim at the gunman and began pulling the trigger again and again. The pistol boomed like thunder, but Tirzah didn't flinch. She knew that her fiancé was in imminent danger and protecting him was her only goal.

The gunman fell to the ground and didn't move. Tirzah assumed that she'd hit him in the head, but she shot him twice more as she approached him for good measure. She wasn't taking any chances.

"Y'all okay?" she asked as the guys rushed out of Rell's Mercedes, drawing their own guns.

Jah kicked the pistol out of the gunman's hand and then leaned over and lifted the black cotton ski mask.

No one seemed surprised to see that it was Johnny B.

He had a hole in the side of his head, another in his neck, and several more in his chest, and he was as dead as he'd intended to leave Jah.

King Rio

Chapter 29

"I, Sincere Jerrell Owens, take you, Tamera Lyon, to be my wife, my partner in life and my one true love. I will cherish our friendship and love you today, tomorrow, and forever. I will trust you and honor you. I will laugh with you and cry with you. I will love you faithfully through the best and the worst, through the difficult and the easy. Whatever may come I will always be there. As I have given you my hand to hold, so I give you my life to keep, so help me God."

Rell's smile burgeoned as he nervously completed his vows. He was gazing into the eyes of his beautiful African American queen, the woman who had stolen his heart on Christmas Eve of last year and had kept it in a warm place ever since.

She looked stunning in her Vera Wang wedding dress, like a princess straight out of blockbuster movie. Her smooth chocolate skin and impeccably applied makeup made her the most beautiful woman he'd ever laid eyes on and he knew now that he wanted to be with her until the end.

"I, Tamera Lyon, take you, Sincere Owens, to be my husband, my partner in life and my one true love. I will cherish our friendship and love you today, tomorrow, and forever. I will trust you and honor you. I will laugh with you and cry with you. I will love you faithfully through the best and the worst, through the difficult and the easy. Whatever may come I will always be there. As I have given you my hand to hold, so I give you my life to keep, so help me God."

Rell was all too happy to finally lift the veil and kiss his bride. He kept his lips pressed to hers for a long minute, ignoring the applause and congratulatory screams. He never thought he'd be as happy as he was at this very moment. After all the ups and downs of life in the cold streets of Chicago, he had finally found a wife.

They were in the ballroom at the Trump International Hotel and Tower. Their families were present, including Tirzah and Jah, who had stood at the very same altar and gotten married just moments prior.

Dora, the ring bearer, was now back on her daddy's lap in the front row of chairs.

The celebrations lasted for half the night, and by the time they left the hotel in a rented Rolls-Royce Phantom with "JUST MARRIED" written across the back window, Rell was halfway drunk and all the way ready for their tropical honeymoon.

They were going to spend the following month on the island of Barbados in a rented villa that was worth $3.7 million and had every amenity they needed to fully enjoy their time together. Tirzah and Jah had a different villa that was just a mile away from theirs.

Tamera and Rell could not keep their hands off each other in the backseat of the Phantom. It took every ounce of restraint Rell possessed not to get an early start on their honeymoon right in front of their driver.

In fact, if the driver wasn't related to Rell, he might have done it and not cared what the driver had to say about it.

"Okay, y'all," Tara said from the driver's seat. She adjusted the rearview mirror to look at them. "We'll be at O'Hare in no less than forty-five minutes. Settle down a bit. Y'all gon' have plenty of time to do all the nasty shit y'all wanna do in a little while."

Tamera snickered and unsealed her lips from Rell's neck, but her hand stayed on the crotch of his pants, massaging the rock-hard pole that was longing for her goodies.

"I'm attacking you as soon as we get on that plane," Tamera said. "We have to go to the bathroom or something. All that champagne got me on ten, I can't even lie."

"Lil hot ass." Rell chuckled and planted a kiss on the tip of her nose. "Just be patient, baby. Wait til we get to the island. That'll make it even better."

Tamera held her hand out to study the engagement ring and wedding band on her finger. Then she brought the hand to her mouth and kissed the massive nine carat diamond.

"You know," Tara said, "Tremaine just got out of the hospital, and he's more fucked up than Apple and Felicia. Way more. He had to have his left leg amputated. He's paralyzed from the waist down because he was shot four times while he was in that trunk and one of the bullets hit his spine. His dick is all messed up. My girl said it's really bad."

"That's what he gets for raping my sister," Tamera said. "Let's see him rape somebody now."

"Yeah, he won't be doing any more of that for a very long time. Probably never again."

Rell looked out the back window at the Bentley that was following them. Tara's husband, K, was driving it, and Jah and Tirzah were in its backseat.

"We won, baby," Rell said, turning to look at Tamera. "We won."

"We did." She lay down on lap and gazed up at him, studying the ring with a dreamy expression on her flawless brown face. "We definitely won. I think we should leave the hood for good now. Now all we gotta do is get Tara and K to move somewhere near us up north and we'll be straight. No more Lawndale for us. No more gunshots and street beefs with other niggas. Zo's dead now, and I doubt if his guys are going to come at you again. They're already badmouthing him for beating up some girl before the police shot him up. He lost the little respect he had in the hood and then lost his life. It's sad, but oh well. It was in God's plan for him to go and it's in God's plan for us to live happily ever after."

"I know that's right, baby." Rell lowered his lips to hers and gave her the most passionate kiss he'd ever given a woman. "Happily ever after is what it's gonna be, baby. Forever and ever."

"I love you, my king."

"And I love you, my queen."

Mr. and Mrs. Owens kissed on each other all the way to the airport.

Epilogue
March 3rd, 2016
10:17 A.M.

"Long as the people in that motherfucker love you dearly
Always gon' be a whip that's better than the one you got
   Always gon' be some clothes that's fresher than the ones you rock
   Always gon' be a bitch that's badder out there on the tours
   But you ain't never gon' be happy till you love yours..."

   The smoothly polished lyrics of J. Cole combined with the warmth of the water in the indoor pool to create the most perfect of scenarios.
   Sitting on the edge of the swimming pool in her one-piece bathing suit with her feet in the water, studying her fingernails and the gleaming diamond ring on her finger and nodding her head to the beat of the music as the sunlight spilled in through the glass roof above, Tamera Owens was at peace. She felt better than she'd ever felt in her life.
   The sound of Rell's body moving gracefully through the water was soothing to her. Last night when they arrived at the villa, they had been much too tired to do much lovemaking, so they had settled for a quickie that set the mood for a nice long sleep, but Rell had awakened her with his mouth on her pussy, and they had made love for over two hours non stop. Looking at her husband swimming through the swimming pool made her want to do it all over again.
   She picked up the iPhone from next to her and recorded a video of him.
   "Rell. Look in the camera," she said.
   He was already swimming toward her. He smiled and blew a kiss at the smartphone.

Tamera turned the camera to herself and said, "We're on our honeymoon in Barbados and this nigga wants to swim in some damn water. You can tell his ass ain't never been no—"

She screamed and dropped her phone as Rell grabbed her feet and acted as if he were getting ready to pull her into the water.

But he quickly let go of her feet and moved in between her thighs. He began kissing on her inner thighs, rubbing his fingertips on the crotch of her bathing suit, looking up at her.

"Asshole," she said.

She got up as he lifted himself out of the pool. Her eyes went to his chest and abdomen. The muscles were so perfect that they could have been drawn on. She ran her fingernails across them and let out a little shout of joy.

"All this for me?" she said, lowering her eyes to the enormous print of his dick behind the black-and-gold Nike swimming trunks he had on. "Mm. And this? Can you say yasssss?"

"Umm, no the fuck I can't say some gay-ass shit like that." Rell laughed and slapped his hands onto Tamera's big soft derrière. "I can give it to you, though. You want it?"

"I always want it." She wrapped her meaty legs around his waist and nibbled on his bottom lip. "I want it now, I want it later — I want it all the time, if that's okay with you."

"That's all you had to say."

He kissed her lips, then her neck, then her breasts. She had expected him to carry her to the bedroom, but he did no such thing. He pushed her legs from around his waist and as soon as her feet hit the floor he hurriedly removed her bathing suit and made her turn her back to him.

He kneeled behind her and dropped his head back before positioning his mouth right up under her pussy.

Tamera quivered when she felt his tongue tap her clitoris and then enter her pussy. She was already wet, and she had not even taken a swim. No, her wetness had come from watching her powerfully built husband move so effortlessly through the water, and remembering how he had fucked her senseless first thing this morning.

She made her ass bounce and shake on his face, knowing how much he liked her to do it. She cupped her breasts in her hands and massaged them while Rell tongued her. It felt so good. He seemed to be getting better and better at pleasing her sexually. His tongue moved like a tornado on her clit, occasionally moving to delve into her before returning to that sensitive spot and continuing to stimulate her until she could no longer take it.

He stood up behind her and put his dick between her ass cheeks. He moved it back and forth and slapped his hands on her ass.

"You ready for this python?" Rell said, running his hands up and around to her breasts.

"Yes," Tamera said.

She bent over and grabbed her ankles, and Rell pushed his thick love muscle in her and gave her exactly what she'd been waiting for.

The End

Submission Guideline

Submit the first three chapters of your completed manuscript to ldpsubmissions@gmail.com, subject line: Your book's title. The manuscript must be in a .doc file and sent as an attachment. Document should be in Times New Roman, double spaced and in size 12 font. Also, provide your synopsis and full contact information. If sending multiple submissions, they must each be in a separate email.

Have a story but no way to send it electronically? You can still submit to LDP/Ca$h Presents. Send in the first three chapters, written or typed, of your completed manuscript to:

LDP: Submissions Dept
Po Box 944
Stockbridge, Ga 30281

DO NOT send original manuscript. Must be a duplicate.

Provide your synopsis and a cover letter containing your full contact information.

Thanks for considering LDP and Ca$h Presents.

NEW RELEASES

MOB TIES 3 by SAYNOMORE
CONFESSIONS OF A GANGSTA by NICHOLAS LOCK
MURDA WAS THE CASE by ELIJAH R. FREEMAN
THE STREETS NEVER LET GO by ROBERT BAPTISTE
MOBBED UP 4 by KING RIO

3X KRAZY III

De'Kari

KINGPIN KILLAZ IV

STREET KINGS III

PAID IN BLOOD III

CARTEL KILLAZ IV

DOPE GODS III

Hood Rich

SINS OF A HUSTLA II

ASAD

RICH $AVAGE II

By Troublesome

YAYO V

Bred In The Game 2

S. Allen

CREAM III

By Yolanda Moore

SON OF A DOPE FIEND III

HEAVEN GOT A GHETTO II

By Renta

LOYALTY AIN'T PROMISED III

By Keith Williams

I'M NOTHING WITHOUT HIS LOVE II

SINS OF A THUG II

TO THE THUG I LOVED BEFORE II

By Monet Dragun

QUIET MONEY IV

EXTENDED CLIP III

THUG LIFE IV

By **Trai'Quan**

THE STREETS MADE ME IV

By **Larry D. Wright**

IF YOU CROSS ME ONCE II

By **Anthony Fields**

THE STREETS WILL NEVER CLOSE II

By K'ajji

HARD AND RUTHLESS III

THE BILLIONAIRE BENTLEYS II

Von Diesel

KILLA KOUNTY II

By Khufu

MONEY GAME II

By Smoove Dolla

A GANGSTA'S KARMA II

By FLAME

JACK BOYZ VERSUS DOPE BOYZ

By Romell Tukes

MOB TIES IV

By SayNoMore

MURDA WAS THE CASE II

Elijah R. Freeman

THE STREETS NEVER LET GO II

By Robert Baptiste

<u>Available Now</u>

RESTRAINING ORDER **I & II**

By **CA$H & Coffee**

LOVE KNOWS NO BOUNDARIES **I II & III**

By **Coffee**

RAISED AS A GOON I, II, III & IV

BRED BY THE SLUMS I, II, III

BLAST FOR ME I & II

ROTTEN TO THE CORE I II III

A BRONX TALE I, II, III

DUFFLE BAG CARTEL I II III IV V VI

HEARTLESS GOON I II III IV V

A SAVAGE DOPEBOY I II

DRUG LORDS I II III

CUTTHROAT MAFIA I II

KING OF THE TRENCHES

By **Ghost**

LAY IT DOWN **I & II**

LAST OF A DYING BREED I II

BLOOD STAINS OF A SHOTTA I & II III

By **Jamaica**

LOYAL TO THE GAME I II III

LIFE OF SIN I, II III

By **TJ & Jelissa**
BLOODY COMMAS I & II
SKI MASK CARTEL I II & III
KING OF NEW YORK I II,III IV V
RISE TO POWER I II III
COKE KINGS I II III IV
BORN HEARTLESS I II III IV
KING OF THE TRAP I II
By **T.J. Edwards**
IF LOVING HIM IS WRONG...I & II
LOVE ME EVEN WHEN IT HURTS I II III
By **Jelissa**
WHEN THE STREETS CLAP BACK I & II III
THE HEART OF A SAVAGE I II III
By **Jibril Williams**
A DISTINGUISHED THUG STOLE MY HEART I II & III
LOVE SHOULDN'T HURT I II III IV
RENEGADE BOYS I II III IV
PAID IN KARMA I II III
SAVAGE STORMS I II
AN UNFORESEEN LOVE
By **Meesha**
A GANGSTER'S CODE I &, II III
A GANGSTER'S SYN I II III
THE SAVAGE LIFE I II III
CHAINED TO THE STREETS I II III
BLOOD ON THE MONEY I II III

By J-Blunt

PUSH IT TO THE LIMIT

By **Bre' Hayes**

BLOOD OF A BOSS **I, II, III, IV, V**

SHADOWS OF THE GAME

TRAP BASTARD

By **Askari**

THE STREETS BLEED MURDER **I, II & III**

THE HEART OF A GANGSTA I II& III

By **Jerry Jackson**

CUM FOR ME I II III IV V VI VII

An **LDP Erotica Collaboration**

BRIDE OF A HUSTLA **I II & II**

THE FETTI GIRLS **I, II& III**

CORRUPTED BY A GANGSTA I, II III, IV

BLINDED BY HIS LOVE

THE PRICE YOU PAY FOR LOVE I, II ,III

DOPE GIRL MAGIC I II III

By **Destiny Skai**

WHEN A GOOD GIRL GOES BAD

By **Adrienne**

THE COST OF LOYALTY I II III

By Kweli

A GANGSTER'S REVENGE **I II III & IV**

THE BOSS MAN'S DAUGHTERS I II III IV V

A SAVAGE LOVE **I & II**

BAE BELONGS TO ME I II

A HUSTLER'S DECEIT I, II, III

WHAT BAD BITCHES DO I, II, III

SOUL OF A MONSTER I II III

KILL ZONE

A DOPE BOY'S QUEEN I II III

By **Aryanna**

A KINGPIN'S AMBITON

A KINGPIN'S AMBITION **II**

I MURDER FOR THE DOUGH

By **Ambitious**

TRUE SAVAGE I II III IV V VI VII

DOPE BOY MAGIC I, II, III

MIDNIGHT CARTEL I II III

CITY OF KINGZ I II

NIGHTMARE ON SILENT AVE

By **Chris Green**

A DOPEBOY'S PRAYER

By **Eddie "Wolf" Lee**

THE KING CARTEL **I, II & III**

By **Frank Gresham**

THESE NIGGAS AIN'T LOYAL **I, II & III**

By **Nikki Tee**

GANGSTA SHYT **I II &III**

By **CATO**

THE ULTIMATE BETRAYAL

By **Phoenix**

BOSS'N UP **I , II & III**

By **Royal Nicole**

I LOVE YOU TO DEATH

By **Destiny J**

I RIDE FOR MY HITTA

I STILL RIDE FOR MY HITTA

By **Misty Holt**

LOVE & CHASIN' PAPER

By **Qay Crockett**

TO DIE IN VAIN

SINS OF A HUSTLA

By **ASAD**

BROOKLYN HUSTLAZ

By **Boogsy Morina**

BROOKLYN ON LOCK I & II

By **Sonovia**

GANGSTA CITY

By **Teddy Duke**

A DRUG KING AND HIS DIAMOND I & II III

A DOPEMAN'S RICHES

HER MAN, MINE'S TOO I, II

CASH MONEY HO'S

THE WIFEY I USED TO BE I II

By Nicole Goosby

TRAPHOUSE KING **I II & III**

KINGPIN KILLAZ I II III

STREET KINGS I II

PAID IN BLOOD **I II**

CARTEL KILLAZ I II III

DOPE GODS I II

By **Hood Rich**

LIPSTICK KILLAH **I, II, III**

CRIME OF PASSION I II & III

FRIEND OR FOE I II III

By **Mimi**

STEADY MOBBN' **I, II, III**

THE STREETS STAINED MY SOUL I II

By **Marcellus Allen**

WHO SHOT YA **I, II, III**

SON OF A DOPE FIEND I II

HEAVEN GOT A GHETTO

Renta

GORILLAZ IN THE BAY **I II III IV**

TEARS OF A GANGSTA I II

3X KRAZY I II

DE'KARI

TRIGGADALE I II III

MURDAROBER WAS THE CASE

Elijah R. Freeman

GOD BLESS THE TRAPPERS I, II, III

THESE SCANDALOUS STREETS I, II, III

FEAR MY GANGSTA I, II, III IV, V

THESE STREETS DON'T LOVE NOBODY I, II

BURY ME A G I, II, III, IV, V

A GANGSTA'S EMPIRE I, II, III, IV

THE DOPEMAN'S BODYGAURD I II

THE REALEST KILLAZ I II III

THE LAST OF THE OGS I II III

Tranay Adams

THE STREETS ARE CALLING

Duquie Wilson

MARRIED TO A BOSS I II III

By Destiny Skai & Chris Green

KINGZ OF THE GAME I II III IV V

Playa Ray

SLAUGHTER GANG I II III

RUTHLESS HEART I II III

By Willie Slaughter

FUK SHYT

By Blakk Diamond

DON'T F#CK WITH MY HEART I II

By Linnea

ADDICTED TO THE DRAMA I II III

IN THE ARM OF HIS BOSS II

By Jamila

YAYO I II III IV

A SHOOTER'S AMBITION I II

BRED IN THE GAME

By S. Allen

TRAP GOD I II III

RICH $AVAGE

By Troublesome

FOREVER GANGSTA

GLOCKS ON SATIN SHEETS I II

By Adrian Dulan

TOE TAGZ I II III

LEVELS TO THIS SHYT I II

By Ah'Million

KINGPIN DREAMS I II III

By Paper Boi Rari

CONFESSIONS OF A GANGSTA I II III IV

By Nicholas Lock

I'M NOTHING WITHOUT HIS LOVE

SINS OF A THUG

TO THE THUG I LOVED BEFORE

By Monet Dragun

CAUGHT UP IN THE LIFE I II III

THE STREETS NEVER LET GO

By Robert Baptiste

NEW TO THE GAME I II III

MONEY, MURDER & MEMORIES I II III

By **Malik D. Rice**

LIFE OF A SAVAGE I II III

A GANGSTA'S QUR'AN I II III

MURDA SEASON I II III

GANGLAND CARTEL I II III

CHI'RAQ GANGSTAS I II III

KILLERS ON ELM STREET I II III

JACK BOYZ N DA BRONX I II III

A DOPEBOY'S DREAM

By **Romell Tukes**

LOYALTY AIN'T PROMISED I II

By Keith Williams

QUIET MONEY I II III

THUG LIFE I II III

EXTENDED CLIP I II

By **Trai'Quan**

THE STREETS MADE ME I II III

By **Larry D. Wright**

THE ULTIMATE SACRIFICE I, II, III, IV, V, VI

KHADIFI

IF YOU CROSS ME ONCE

ANGEL I II

IN THE BLINK OF AN EYE

By **Anthony Fields**

THE LIFE OF A HOOD STAR

By Ca$h & Rashia Wilson

THE STREETS WILL NEVER CLOSE

By K'ajji

CREAM I II

By Yolanda Moore

NIGHTMARES OF A HUSTLA I II III

By King Dream

CONCRETE KILLA I II

By Kingpen

HARD AND RUTHLESS I II

MOB TOWN 251

THE BILLIONAIRE BENTLEYS

By Von Diesel

GHOST MOB

Stilloan Robinson

MOB TIES I II III

By SayNoMore

BODYMORE MURDERLAND I II III

By Delmont Player

FOR THE LOVE OF A BOSS

By C. D. Blue

MOBBED UP I II III IV

By King Rio

KILLA KOUNTY

By Khufu

MONEY GAME

By Smoove Dolla

A GANGSTA'S KARMA

By FLAME

BOOKS BY LDP'S CEO, CA$H

TRUST IN NO MAN

TRUST IN NO MAN 2

TRUST IN NO MAN 3

BONDED BY BLOOD

SHORTY GOT A THUG

THUGS CRY

THUGS CRY 2

THUGS CRY 3

TRUST NO BITCH

TRUST NO BITCH 2

TRUST NO BITCH 3

TIL MY CASKET DROPS

RESTRAINING ORDER

RESTRAINING ORDER 2

IN LOVE WITH A CONVICT

LIFE OF A HOOD STAR

King Rio